JOHN THE PUPIL

John the Pupil

A NOVEL

DAVID FLUSFEDER

HARPER ● PERENNIAL

NEW YORK ● LONDON ● TORONTO ● SYDNEY ● NEW DELHI ● AUCKLAND

HARPER ● PERENNIAL

First published in Great Britain in 2014 by Fourth Estate, an imprint of
HarperCollins Publishers.

A hardcover edition of this book was published in 2015 by HarperCollins
Publishers.

HarperCollins books may be purchased for educational, business, or sales promo-
tional use. For information please e-mail the Special Markets Department at
SPsales@harpercollins.com.

FIRST HARPER PERENNIAL EDITION PUBLISHED 2016.

The Library of Congress has catalogued the hardcover edition as follows:

Flusfeder, D. L., 1960–
   John the pupil : a novel / David Flusfeder.—First edition.
       pages ; cm
    ISBN 978-0-06-233918-8 (hardcover) — ISBN 978-0-06-233919-5 (softcover)—
ISBN 978-0-06-233921-8 (ebook) 1. Monks—Fiction. 2. Middle Ages—Fiction. 3.
Voyages and travels—Fiction. 4. Europe—History—476-1492—Fiction. I. Title.
   PR6056.L77J64 2015
   823'.914—dc23

                                          2014022666

16   17   18   19   20   OV/RRD   10   9   8   7   6   5   4   3   2   1

for brother Mathew

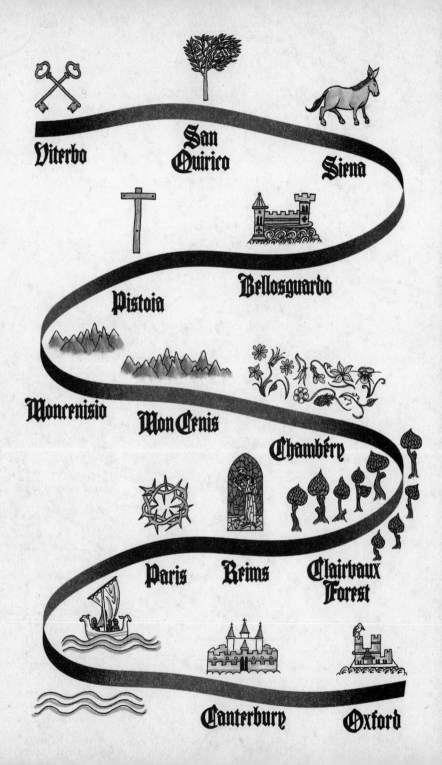

Viterbo

San Quirico

Siena

Bellosguardo

Pistoia

Moncenisio

Mon Cenis

Chambéry

Paris

Reims

Clairvaux Forest

Canterbury

Oxford

Contents

Every point on the earth is the apex of a pyramid filled with the force of the heavens.

ROGER BACON, *Opus Majus*

He shall pass into strange countries: for he shall try good and evil among men.

Ecclesiasticus 39:5

Note on the Text

A few remarks should be made here about the history of this unique manuscript.

I quote from Augustus Jessopp's lecture 'Village Life Six Hundred Years Ago', first delivered to a notoriously uninterested audience in the Public Reading Room of the village of Tittleshall in Norfolk, and later collected in his *The Coming of the Friars and Other Historical Essays* (1885):

> In the autumn of 1878, while on a visit at Rougham Hall, Norfolk, the seat of Mr. Charles North, my kind host drew my attention to some large boxes of manuscripts, which he told me nobody knew anything about, but which I was at liberty to ransack to my heart's content. I at once dived into one of the boxes, and then spent half the night in examining some of its treasures.
>
> The smaller strips of parchment or vellum – for the most part conveyances of land, and having seals attached – have been roughly bound together in volumes, each containing about one hundred documents, and arranged with some regard to chronology, the undated ones being collected into a volume by

themselves. I think it almost certain that the arranging of the early charters in their rude covers was carried out before 1500 A.D., and I have a suspicion that they were grouped together by Sir William Yelverton, 'the cursed Norfolk Justice' of the Paston Letters, who inherited the estate from his mother in the first half of the fifteenth century.

They had lain forgotten until they came under my notice. Of this large mass of documents I had copied or abstracted scarcely more than five hundred, and I had not yet got beyond the year 1355. The court rolls, bailiffs' accounts, and early leases, I had hardly looked at when this lecture was delivered.

It was in this last collection, which the genial eye of the schoolmaster-essayist-cleric Jessopp failed to apprehend, where the fragmented chronicle of John the Pupil lay buried.

Not until another generation after Jessopp were the first attempts made to piece the chronicle together. It is a great shame that the task did not fall to someone more skilled than the amateur antiquarian Gerald Lovelace, whose expertise did not match his enthusiasm. He succeeded in pasting the fragments together in double columns in some kind of chronological order but, robust as parchment is, many of the pages suffered in the process. He presented the 'finished' volume, whose translation he did not attempt, to the benefactress Celia (Cornwell) Bechstein. It has had an unlucky subsequent history, and here is not the place to detail or dwell on its misfortunes and depredations, the estate disputes, the book thieves, the fire at Chatham; until recently it had been stored, in harsh conditions, in a warehouse room in Ealing.

The text before you is a translation from a mixture of languages – primarily Latin, but also some Middle English,

Old French, Italian, and Occitan, as well as Hebrew and Greek. Efforts have been made to preserve the spirit and voice of the original, at the expense, inevitably, of some of the literal meaning.

I have operated under etymological constraints, using only words that would have been known to John or are English cognates to his Latin ones. I may not use the word 'succeed', for example, other than to denote a sequence, because that is a secular, originally sixteenth-century term, which presumes to credit a favourable outcome to an individual's capacities rather than to the divine will. A donkey's ears cannot 'flap'; our companions may not 'embark' or 'struggle' or use 'effort'. When trying to find unanachronistic correlatives for John's vocabulary, I have aimed not for the striking word or phrase, but the most apt and, in most cases, recognisable.

Where there are sections lost from the original manuscript, their absence has been marked by ellipses and blank space.

Most of the fragments follow an obvious chronology (helped by their author's habit of dating each entry by reference to the saint to whom the day is dedicated). One of the harder parts of the editorial task has been to decide upon the arrangement of some of the others. The mistakes that have been made here are the editor-translator's own: I am not a historian or a philologist, just a worker in language, whose path to John's manuscript has been an unlikely one that need not interrupt the reader's attention.

The original has now found a hospitable home in the library of a private collector, who commissioned this translation and provided me with a transcription of the original in the interest of making this extraordinary story available to its widest possible audience, and to whom unutterable thanks are due but hard to bestow, as he wishes to preserve his anonymity.

The Chronicle of John the Pupil

Being the reconstituted fragments of the account of the journey taken by John the Pupil and two companions, at the behest of the friar and magus Roger Bacon, from Oxford to Viterbo in A.D. 1267, carrying secret burden to His Holiness Clement IV, written by himself and detailing some of the difficulties and temptations endured along the way.

... and see your face on the roof of the friary. Sometimes you would cast your eye down at us and we would scatter. More often, the face would disappear as if it had never been there at all, as if you were something we had conjured to frighten ourselves with. He was a prisoner, it was said, convicted of monstrous crimes. He was mad, he fed on the flesh of children, he wiped his mouth with his beard after he had done feasting. He was in league with the Devil, he was the Devil, performing unnatural investigations. Sometimes we would hear inexplicable thunder from the tower, a few claimed to have seen lightning on clear sunny days. Once, by myself, grazing my father's goats, I was touched by a rainbow, slowly turning, painting the field with brief marvellous colour.

As I got older, I would go there less often. The grass grew higher by that part of the Franciscans' wall. Strange flowers bloomed. Animals refused to graze there.

Most of the commerce of our village, maybe all the commerce, was done with the friars. They bought our milk and cheese and mutton, we cut down trees to sell for firewood. Sometimes we would catch sight of their Minister walking to Oxford. We would see the friars at mass. They came to preach to us. And, when I was about nine years old, two of the friars came to our village and gathered the children in a circle by the pond. They asked us questions about numbers and words, they instructed us to wield their shapes, and gave us apples in exchange for the correct answers. At the end, I had by far the most apples.

The following day, they came for me. I had no part of the transaction. When it was done, my father seemed satisfied. I hope he got a good price for me.

And so began my education. In the tower at the top of the friary where, Master Roger, you have your seclusion and your books – twenty or more when I arrived, an immense library to which you proceeded to add, bought through means I never did discover. It was not just me at first in that room of books and instruments and crystal and glass, there were other boys lifted from villages who had also passed the apple test.

You taught us the trivium, the arts of grammar, rhetoric and dialectic, and the quadrivium, which are the arts of arithmetic, geometry, astronomy and music.

You read Aristotle to us, so much Aristotle, the ways of the heavens and the beasts of the field, Aristotle on Categories, on Prior and Posterior Analytics, the Sophistical Refutations. And you read Porphyry to us, and Nicomachus of Gerasa, and John of Sacrobosco, and the Elements of Euclid and the Practical Geometry of Leonardo of Pisa because, Master Roger, you said geometry is the foremost instrument for the demonstration of theological truth as well as being necessary for the understanding of natural philosophy.

The class shrunk, boys were cast aside, sent back to their villages, or given occupations elsewhere in the friary. And we read Grosseteste on light and Boethius on music, and Ptolemy on Astronomy, and Aristotle again, on the Heavens and Meteorology, on Plants, on Metaphysics.

4

And we read Qusta ibn Luqa on the Difference between Soul and Spirit and Averroes on geometry, and the antique authors of Rome: Seneca on the passions, Ovid on the transformations. You had taught in Paris, you used your lecture notes from the time before you had become a friar, and the class further shrank, my companions were too dull, too slow, they could not compute, deduce, dispute to our Master's satisfaction, no matter how loudly you read or how hard you drove your wisdom against their bodies and souls.

For your primary method of pedagogy was to beat the information into your students' heads: Here are the examples, numbers 1, 2 and 3. What are the examples?– *Beat!* – What are the examples?! List them! – Good enough. Now what law do these examples illustrate and prove? – *Beat!* – What are the examples? – Yes. Now what laws do they illustrate? – Yes. Now again. And again.

Your other method was to offer a short description of a special case in nature. It was the pupil's work to gather this new information into what he already had been taught, to offer up a law to account for this otherwise strange manifestation, and the craft would be to form an argument so fine that it would entice you, Master Roger, elsewhere now, unmindful, back into the dispute.

(And, in the schoolroom, when they thought they were unobserved and unheard, Brother Luke would maliciously lead his fellows in a recitation of the martyrdom of Saint Felix, the strict teacher whose pupils stabbed him to death with their pens.)

Elsewhere, I saw little of the friary and nothing of the world. The friars went out to the city to preach, while my work was to learn. And then there were just two of us, me and Daniel, whose understanding was just as nimble, perhaps even nimbler than my own, but had an impediment which sometimes kept the required answers hidden behind eyes that were too large for his body, and we were the last vessels for my Master's knowledge. Occasionally, on the roof, constructing the apparatus for the burning mirror, I would see my former classmates and the novice friars below. I once saw Brother Andrew and Brother Bernard nursing a broken-winged starling, but my Master called me back before I could discover if their labours prospered. I attended prayers. Each day, before Vespers, I had an hour for myself when I would lie on my bed, and meditate, try to quench the triangles and squares that occupied my inner vision and fight the demons that grow so strong before daylight, and bring myself closer to the steps of Our Lord, and otherwhile try to remember how my life used to be.

In this way were my days sanctified. In this way did I give thanks to the God who made me and the Saviour who redeemed me.

· · ·

My Master does not approve of the divisions of the seasons. My Master does not approve of many things or, indeed, people. He disapproves of Peter of Lombardy and Thomas Aquinas and Albertus Magnus and the translators of the Holy Scriptures who have incorporated so many errors into the sacred text. He disapproves of the Principals of our Order who have sacrificed the lamb of knowledge on the altar of temporal concerns. He disapproves of anyone who does not believe the evidence of his own eyes and takes no pains to celebrate the glory of creation by gathering knowledge to gain a closer apprehension of God's work.

My Master holds the wisdom of his own teacher Robert Grosseteste to be above all others in the present age, but even he is not beyond reproach as in his acceptance of the division of the seasons into four, when it should be, rather, three, intervals of growth, equilibrium and decline. My Master also has proved that the calendar is wrong. By his calculations, one-hundred-and-one-thirtieth of a day is being lost every year, as our method of reckoning the passage of time loses pace with the rhythms of the stars.

· · ·

And I would help him build his mirrors and lenses, my instruction would proceed, and he would beat out time and we would sing together, and the fallacious seasons passed, and the misreckoned years passed, and I was seventeen years old and the only one left in his classroom.

Saint Athanasius's Day

Brother Andrew so dainty and girlish, Brother Bernard silent and large and phlegmatic, half-doltish. Brother Luke the reprobate, malicious and acting so freely, and somehow, his lightness, always escaping censure. Perhaps this is because he has the ear of the sacristan. Brother Daniel is the perpetual mark for Brother Luke. There is a quality about Brother Daniel that offends Brother Luke, and rouses his energies. Brother Daniel takes these attentions without complaint, as if they are his due. He humbly bears the weight of Brother Luke's tricks.

At night I go to sleep listening to the murmur of this little herd of novices in the dormitory at night as they devise their wiles against Brother Daniel. They do not include Brothers

Andrew or Bernard in their works. Brother Andrew would be their mark were it not for the greater offence that Brother Daniel causes them. Brother Bernard stands neither for nor against them. They regard him as a beast in the field, not quite man.

As for me, they do not dare to act directly. They whisper against me too, I hear them, on walks down to the refectory, to mass; but the fear of Master Roger's mystery and power extends to me: just as in those days of living outside the walls, when we looked up to the friary tower to frighten ourselves and fear you and throw little stones that would not reach a quarter of the way to the roof, not daring to look over our shoulders as we ran away to the safety of our fathers' world, in case we saw demons flying after us, they dislike me but they do not dare to assault me in case Master Roger's power move itself against them.

• • •

You ask me to observe the world, and you are my world, so I shall begin with you.

Master Roger is well-made. His body is strong, putting to shame the constitutions of men half his age. His eyes are the colour of the sea on a stormy spring morning. His beard is grey. He credits his strength and vigour to his diet. The purpose, he says, in eating and drinking, is to satisfy the desires of nature, not to fill and empty the stomach. He has his own elixirs of rhubarb and black hellebore, which he pounds down to a paste and adds to his meat. And I have mine, justly accorded to my age and capacities. My Master says that if I observe the regimen he lays down I might live as long as the nature assumed from my parents might permit. It is only the corruption of my father and his fathers before him that limits the utmost term beyond which I may not pass.

Master Roger does not sleep in the dormitory. Master Roger does not take his meals with the rest of the friary. Master Roger appears at most services, space around him separating him from the rest of the Order, his voice sonorous, distinct, godly. The remainder of the time he is in his room at the top of the tower, performing his investigations.

Our lessons are fewer, now that he is working so hard on his Great Work. But still, towards the end of each day, he will test me on the knowledge that he has poured into me, and then add a little more. I must answer his questions about mathematics and music and grammar and rhetoric and optics, demonstrate the burning mirror he has made; and if my answers are not full and prompt, if my demonstration is not performed with his subtlety and skill, if I do not speak with as much insight and wit as if he were the respondent, he beats correction into my head.

Humbly, I observe myself. I am of smaller stature than my Master. My limbs are narrow and may not carry great loads. When I observe my own features they do not displease me, but they are not yet full. On occasion I am told by one of the older friars to walk with greater solemnity because my body, if not countermanded, tends to rise with every step.

I am the mirror he is constructing, to reflect him back to himself.

· · ·

Our steps are directed by the Lord. I had no choice in this, nor should I have. Who is the man that can understand his own way? But all the same, in the order of our days, in the book of our hours, as I perform my spiritual exercises, my mind wanders. As Cassian has written, we try to bind the mind fast with chains and it slips away swifter than a snake.

Once, when I was very young, there was a traveller, a Frenchman, who visited the friary. He spoke of mountains and kings and far places and aroused my Master's envy, but also his respect. He had visited Tartars and Saracens and travelled in carts pulled by giant dogs that had the ferocity of lions. The traveller's skin had been burnt in eastern deserts; his right hand was missing two fingers. He made mention of other injuries but as his body and much of his head were covered by a dark cloak we could only conjecture what they might have been. When he spoke, some of his sentences fell away before finding their conclusion, and he looked silently past those assembled as if part of him were still dwelling in a far place.

In front of me there is a map of the pilgrim way from Canterbury to Jerusalem by way of Rome. The journey does not signify an actual one, I know that. The purpose of this exercise is to lift the spirit into closer fellowship with Our Lord. Imagining myself on this pilgrim route, I walk towards the celestial city, stepping closer into the tread of the Redeemer as he laboured under the Cross.

It is in contemplation that the Christian finds the true Jerusalem.

Demons tempt me away. A demon of vanity drives me to demonstrate my own cleverness. Another demon pulls with his fingers at my cloak tugging me away from Our Lord, whispering to me about the false, earthly road.

I look into the rivers, the sea, the towers of the cities. I trace my fingers along the vellum and hope, forlornly, sinfully, for an actual journey, to take bodily steps along an actual road, a strange sun on my skin, dip my feet, not my fingers on ink, into a changing water.

The rivers and the sea are inscribed in azure. The writer who drew the map is at work most of the days, and nights, sleepless and secret, because my Master needs him for his Great Work. The map is unfinished. The imaginary pilgrim may not travel to the Holy Land because the map stops short of Rome. The sea disappears and the land becomes sky because the scribe suffers from a need to draw lines and curves with azure in the margins of my Master's work.

I inscribe this on cuttings of parchment from my Master's Great Work. At the end of the day, I sweep away the shreds from around the scribe's desk and take what I require for my own work, a humble mockery of the true work. I do not think my Master begrudges me a little ink to make an account of my days.

Saint Abran's Day

Once I knew how to herd goats, to fetch water without losing a drop, to make myself small against my father's anger. Now I have become skilled in the art of gliding through the refectory and kitchen, to pick up bread, to lean over candlesticks and slice off small segments at the base of the candles, and on through the building, to the stairs, my arms folded, hands holding my spoils in the sleeves of my cloak. Our scribe needs food to eat and light to work by.

It is harder to gather wine and beer. When I descend into the cellar, to tiptoe past sleeping Brother Mark, to lift away two bottles, to make my return journey past the sleeping sentinel, to climb back up into the corridor by the dormitory, I am almost as anxious as I used to be, when I first followed Master Roger's instruction to fetch food for the scribe. I know that it is not stealing, he explained to me that it is not, but still I shake, and pray. I must take two bottles, because when Brother Mark makes his accounting of the cellar, he touches each bottle in turn, chanting, sing-song, *Here is master bottle and here is his wife, here is master bottle and here is his wife...* His reckoning is done by remembering whether there was an even or an odd quantity of bottles on the previous day.

The scribe bemoans as he transcribes. He is being made to work too swiftly. It is the word, not its shape, that matters, Master Roger tells him, urging him on, *Faster! Faster!* I have written in the Book, in a rougher hand than the scribe's, because Master Roger did not trust the scribe to draw Hebrew characters without understanding. Maybe, somewhere, a family is missing its father, a mother her son. The scribe shapes an azure line in the margin, he cannot help himself, a turn of thin colour that suggests the tip of a wave, a leafy branch of a tree. He sharpens his pen and wipes his face and looks around, as if for escape. There is none. He is here until the Book is finished or the world has ended.

Or if the Principal discovers what Master Roger is doing in his room. There is an Interdiction cruelly upon him. He may not write or debate or disseminate, other than sequestered in the friary classroom with his appointed pupil. The Order suspects him of novelties, which is an accusation hardly short of heresy. Yet he may exchange letters with friends and outside patrons of influence whom the Principal and even the Minister General should not seek to offend. Master Roger's rooms are turned into a single industry. It is ail done in the utmost secrecy. The Book is secret, which is maybe as it should be. In antique times, Master Aristotle composed a commentary to kingship, power and wisdom for his pupil Alexander of Macedonia. Master Roger's Great Work is the true successor to Aristotle's Secret of Secrets. Many evils follow the man who reveals secrets, wrote Aristotle. The planets align, the Principal vexes, Master Roger writes the words on wax tablets for transcription, the scribe cuts them into the page. I steal a wheel of cheese from the cellar and draw an imaginary journey before picking up my own pen.

We live in the Last Days. All things are temporary. The gates behind which Alexander enclosed Gog and Magog are falling. The horsemen are already abroad. In which case, I asked my Master, why should he, should we, make so many terrible labours to produce his Book? It is a work of majesty, indisputably, a magnificence of learning and opinion and ingenious device, which tells of the world and how it is viewed and the arc of the rainbow and the movements of the stars and of health and immortality and engines of war, all manners of things that would seem miraculous were they not founded on observation and deduction and Scripture, but, even if it is finished, even if it is somehow delivered and received by its intended Reader, would it not be for nothing? All things are known to the angels. They should not need to read it. And, as it has been written, the spread of learning will itself hasten the End Times. My Master hit me across the head with his Greek Grammar and commanded me to read and memorise the declensions of forty-nine nouns. It was as if I had accused him of vanity and pride, and maybe, thoughtlessly, I had.

Saint Epimachus's Day

The winding blue lines of the scribe's demon entered my dreams last night. They became a river in Eden, branches of the Tree, our Beginning as well as an End. I wonder what takes place in Master Roger's dreams, whether he permits himself to imagine figures without end.

There was trouble in the dormitory again. But I watched without attention. The day was so similar to the previous day, as it will be to the next. We beseech you O Lord, that the virtue of the Holy Spirit may be present unto us: which may mildly both purge our hearts, and also defend us from all adversities, through Our Lord Jesus Christ your Son: Who lives and reigns, God, with you, in the unity of the Holy Ghost, world without end.

. . .

Saint John the Silent's Day

The scribe's hand shakes, the pages are almost filled. His escape is close at hand. Master Roger is almost merry. His Great Work is nearly made.

And now, he said, we must talk about how we are going to deliver it.

We? I said.

The proscription is absolute against his leaving this friary which is his prison. For a moment my heart had leapt at the thought of accompanying my Master on a journey; but then I took his meaning as being abstract, that he was generously acknowledging my small part in his Work's manufacture and kindly including me in a conversation about the method of its delivery.

You, he said.

Perhaps he mistook my silence for misapprehension, or fear, or simple stupidity.

You, he repeated. You are the only one I can trust. You will take it to the Pope.

A special mark of favour, an answering heart, or just the fate that the Lord bestows upon us somehow miraculously accords with what I most yearn for.

You will go in three days, he said. The day and the stars are propitious. Ten plus seven.

Numbers of perfection, I said.

You will have companions, Master Roger said.

Companions?

The journey is too difficult for one boy to complete on his own. Do you have friends here? Whom do you trust?

Despite my exhilaration, I was suddenly sad. I felt friend-less, alone. Other than Master Roger, whom it would be an awful presumption to claim for a friend, I have no intimates, no ties of true affection. I have lived in this place for seven years and more and established no bonds of love. Maybe the journey will not be the thing of glory I have dreamed of, maybe there will just be the perpetual here and now, we carry with us the stain and the mark. And I was jealous too. This mission is too grand, too enormous to share.

Who are your friends? There will be three of you.

I thought of the dormitory I sleep in, the novices at play. I looked at the faces my recollection brought to mind, the companions I would not tire of, the friends I would like to share my adventures with, and my heart.

Brothers Andrew and Bernard, I said.

It shall be done, he said. And you will proceed with your writing to make a chronicle of your journey.

How he knows of my secret writing, I do not know. I bowed my head.

Yes, I said.

And you will collect these treasures along your way.

He gave me a list of the things I will be seeking. He also gave me a stack of parchment and three pens and a pot of ink for my writing.

But do not tarry. If it is a choice between the speed of your journey and the search for these treasures, stay on your road.

Yes, I said.

The way will be hard. You have so little experience of the world. The Devil extends his power into unlikely places. There are demons who look like men.

Yes, I said.

And women, he said.

Yes, I said.

God will direct you.

Yes.

He saw there was something that I needed to say. He asked me what it was.

My father, I said, who lives in the village. I have not seen him in five years. I would like to take leave of him before I go.

My Master did not say anything. He turned away.

Downstairs, life proceeded as it always does, as if the world had not changed. Vigils, Lauds, Prime, Terce, Nones, Vespers, Compline. The sun rises, sets, rises again. We pray, give thanks, eat, drink, purge, sleep. God is good. The friary walls are cold against the skin.

Saint Brendan's Day

Saint Brendan, the holy, sailed east with fourteen monks to find the island of paradise that prophecy had promised him. They sailed, in God's name, and found the Island of Sheep by the Mountain of Stone, and they sailed on to an island on which the sailors lit their cauldron to prepare their food, but the island began to move and it was no island, but the great fish Jascoyne, which labours day and night to put its tail in its mouth, but may not, because of its great size, and the sailors fled and sailed fast away.

And they landed on a fair island full of flowers and herbs and trees in which were great birds that sang all the hours of prayer; and they sailed on through tempests and trials to the island of holy monks who do not speak, and in mark of their great holiness have an angel to light the candles in their church; and they sailed on and fought great beasts of the sea and, through God's will, escaped an island of fire inhabited by demons who strode across the water to assault them with burning hooks and burning hammers; and they met the great traitor Judas, naked, fleshless, beaten by the winds and the sea; and they met Saint Paul on the island on which he dwelled for forty years, without meat or drink; and on they sailed, through a dark mist to the fairest and most temperate country a man might see, all of its trees charged with ripe fruit, and precious gems scattered across the ground, and a river which no man might cross. They plucked their fill of the fruit and they gathered as many gems as they would, and all was replenished, for this was Paradise; and they sailed back to their abbey in Ireland, from which they had been gone seven years. Shortly afterwards, Saint Brendan, the holy, the mariner, full of virtues, departed from this life to the one everlasting.

Consternation in the friary. Murmurs in the refectory, heads bowed in sharp telling. During the service of Vigils looks of pity and wonder were sent my way. After Lauds, I was summoned into the Principal's rooms. Seldom have I spoken with the Principal. On a few occasions I have performed for him, for my Master to demonstrate my knowledge and, therefore, his pedagogy. I have always disliked these occasions, standing lonely and cold, unfriendly curious eyes upon me, to make recitations of Greek mathematics, of the houses of the constellations. I have never been in his rooms before. The Principal is a large man who has no love for Master Roger. He asked me what I had to say for myself. I had nothing to say because it did not seem opportune to demonstrate my command of tongues, ancient and present, or to recite my recent lessons in geometry and the nature of light.

These are heavy crimes you are accused of, he said.

Of what am I accused?

It would be best to tell all.

When I first made confession, I lied. I could not think of any sins to confess, so I invented some, gaining a consolation that at least on my following confession, I could confess to the sin of lying while making confession. But this was different. Was it my Master? Had the Principal learned of the Great Work, of the Mission to the Pope? Had the scribe reported of his imprisonment and labours? Did the Principal know of my part in the breaking of the Interdiction?

It had been an act of pride to think that I could deliver the Great Work to the Pope. If I was so stuttering and undone with the Principal, it was unthinkable that I might ever presume to be in the presence of the Vicar of Rome.

I have been guilty of the sin of pride, I said.

Never mind that. Let me smell your breath.

The Principal pulled me over to him roughly by the arm. A second time, he commanded me to breathe on him, which reluctantly I did. His own odour was not good, it tasted like neglected meat.

Again, he said.

I breathed on him again. He thrust me away.

This proves nothing, he said. You will have to perform penance. You and the other two.

I did not understand the purpose or meaning of the test by breath. But his reference to my two associates further strengthened my assumption that he was referring to Master Roger and the wretched scribe. We had broken the rules of our Order, of the blessed Saint Francis, of whom the Principal is a shadow. I was not concerned for myself. Happily, I would have taken all the blame but it could hardly be believed that it was I who had led my Master astray.

I will be taking counsel in prayer now. Tell the other malefactors to visit me after Prime.

He looked at me. I said nothing, deciding that in silence I should least harm my Master.

You will tell them.

Of course, My Lord. But, who?

Brothers Andrew and Bernard. Tell them to visit me.

I returned to the dormitory, gathered my writing materials and went into the shadow of the far wall that stands closest to my former village, where I write this now. I thought I detected the hand of my Master in this. I had not thought him malicious or vengeful. Was it because I expressed a desire to take leave of my father? But I could not believe he would take this kind of action against me, or threaten the mission to deliver his Book to His Holiness the Pope, or indeed make martyrs of Brothers Andrew or Bernard, sacrifice the innocents as well as his Great Work on a spiteful altar.

Incline, O Mother of Mercy, the ears of your pity unto my unworthy supplications, and be unto me, a most wretched sinner, a pious helper in all things.

My Master was delighted. He rubbed his hands together. His eyes shimmered.

So, you have got yourself in trouble, he said.

I do not know what I am supposed to have done.

You have been stealing wine from the cellar.

But I did this for you.

You did not tell them that.

I did not know what I was accused of, and nor would I have betrayed you even if I had.

You are a good boy, he said.

And then he beat my head with his hand, an action which hurt me but did not grieve me because I understood that it was an act of tenderness and acts of tender affection do not come easily to Master Roger.

Because you are my charge, I have been permitted to decide upon the penance that will be required of you to expiate your sin. I believe that they think it right, perhaps restorative, that one under an Interdiction be put into the position of a judge. They have even permitted me to determine how to dispose of your fellows.

But they are not guilty.

Are we not all guilty? Did we not all participate in the sin of the Fall?

I have never known my Master like this, so light and careless.

Be that as it may, he said. I am going to make an unorthodox judgement in your cases. The Principal will accept it. I have decided that this crime is so great, its cupidity, its incontinence and greed, the gluttony it indicates, the treachery against your Franciscan brothers, these sins are all so large that nothing less than a pilgrimage would suffice to pardon them.

My Master was smiling. His beard parted to reveal the paleness of his tongue, the yellow of his teeth. He reached his arm towards me but I was quicker this time and prepared for it and able to escape it this time.

Slowly, the grace of understanding was being granted me.

And where are we to go? I said feeling an answering smile on my own face.

For these extraordinary crimes, my Master said wiping his mouth with his hand, it is deemed that nothing less is required than for you to travel abroad to his Holiness to ask forgiveness of the Pope.

How? How did you order this?

But my Master was laughing, and when he had stopped laughing, his mirth had been discharged.

You will set out as we discussed. We have some preparations to make for your travels.

I am going to Rome?

Not Rome. The Papal court is in Viterbo. There is strife in Rome.

And then he looked at me and around the room, the books, the crystals, the boxes of herbs, the scribe's table bearing the drips of his ink and the scars of his pen, the four packets wrapped in heavy cloth that contain the seven parts of the Great Work; and then he looked back at me again and reached for me and held me to his breast and stroked my hair in a powerful and strange charity and whispered that there was strife everywhere and he wished me good fortune on the road I had ahead of me.

Saint Restituta's Day

It is said that, From a clear spring, clear waters flow. A man is estimated by the company he keeps. Brothers Andrew, Bernard and I stood outside the friary. Master Roger kept reiterating the details of my mission. You will tell the Pope this, and this, and you will demonstrate the device to him, and you will insist upon the need for a more satisfactory translation of the Bible.

The details of my mission are written on my memory. I had no need to be instructed in any of them.

And you will take this bag for the gathering of treasures. And here is parchment for you to write on. If you find the opportunity, send communication to me. And you remember the details of your itinerary?

I remember.

Our Great Work is in this box. Do not dare open it.

The bag for treasure is a heavy cloth one, the sort the villagers use to gather the harvest of apples. The box is made of wood and stained a dark red colour like blood. A single green stone is set into its lid and green wax seals it shut.

Do not open it. Promise me you will not open it.

I will not open it.

And you will carry this also.

He gave me this final load without care, wrapped in linen and tied with twine.

You will open this only when you have given up all hope. You understand me?

The extra packet is heavy at the bottom of the sack I carry, further cloth around it with my bowl and spoon and knife and parchment and styluses wrapped inside. The device I am to demonstrate to the Pope and the box containing the Great Work are in Brother Bernard's sack.

I implore divine mercy that He Who is the One, the beginning and the ending, Alpha and Omega, might join a good end to a good beginning by a safe middle, my Master said.

Brother Bernard is eternally phlegmatic. He stood there, ox-like, bearing the burden of our load. Brother Andrew looked as anxious as I must have done. He shivered, his eyes closing and opening and closing against the sunshine. Suddenly, the prospect of a journey was a matter of trepidation. I had never been outside the village and the friary, except on the wings of Master Roger's knowledge, and during my imaginary journeys. The friars gathered at the gate, Master Roger wiped away something that was occluding his eyes, and the Principal gave the blessing of the Sarum Missal.

The almighty and everlasting God, Who is the Way, the Truth, and the Life, dispose your journey according to His good will; send his angel Raphael to keep you in this your pilgrimage, and both lead you in peace on your way to the place where you would be, and bring you back again on your return to us in safety.

And so our journey began. We walked past the village on the way to the river. I fancied I saw my father in a field beating a goat.

Saint Helena's Day

The wood of the cross was a vile wood, because crosses used for crucifixions were made of vile wood. It was an unfruitful wood, because no matter how many such trees were planted on the mount of Calvary, the wood gave no fruit. It was a low wood, because it was used for the execution of criminals; a wood of darkness, because it was dark and without any beauty; a wood of death, because on it men were put to death; a malodorous wood, because it was planted among cadavers. After Christ's passion what had been low became sublime. Its stench became an odour of sweetness. Darkness turns to light. As Augustine says, The cross, which was the gibbet of criminals, has made its way to the foreheads of emperors. As Chrysostom says, Christ's cross and his scars will, on the Day of Judgement, shine more brightly than the sun's rays.

After the murder of Our Lord, the Romans built a temple to Venus on Golgotha, so that any Christian praying there would be seen to be worshipping Venus. When Saint Helena, wife of the first Constantine, mother of the second, came to Jerusalem to find the True Cross, she commanded the temple to be razed, the earth to be ploughed up, and three crosses were disinterred, because Christ had been crucified beside two thieves. To distinguish between the crosses, she had them placed in the centre of Jerusalem and Saint Helena waited for the Lord to manifest his glory. At about the ninth hour, a funeral procession was going past. The dead man's body was placed beneath each of the crosses, and beneath the third cross, the dead man came back to life.

•

The way cuts into us. Pebbles and twigs assail our feet, branches lash our faces and eyes. Our stops for rest are more frequent than I should have liked. The sun moves fast in the heavens; our feet go slowly on the ground. After the exhilaration of setting off on our journey when we took too fast a pace, stung by the novelty of strange trees and different faces, our bodies protested the labour. To Viterbo? To Paris? Canterbury, even Rochester would seem impossible. By the end of the day the next-but-one step would seem impossible.

Brother Bernard hardly speaks. He grunts when he walks, our beast of burden, our donkey. It is forbidden to members of our Order to ride. It is also forbidden to carry. We carry and yet refuse to ride, when a passing merchant or farmer offers us room in his cart, as if resisting a second sin obviates the first already committed. We are not pilgrims, or penitents, we are on a mission to the Pope, but my companions, who are ignorant of the true reason for our journey, refuse to break the saint's commandment. They are both perplexed by their supposed crime and banishment. Neither, I think, is unhappy to have left the friary. Brother Andrew's good nature emerges in whistling and song and an excited regard of everything he sees.

We walk. We accept alms from strangers who have sins to expiate. We walk in the same rhythm. The road we walked on was wide. And there were others on it too, I had never seen such diversity of kinds. Farmers driving their pigs, merchants in carts, cattle for market grazing by the side. And sometime a fine horseman would gallop past down the middle of the road. And we would gaze upon the finery and the speed and the hoof prints left in the mud and the steam disturbing the air.

Towards the end of the day, we had been singing to forget

the pain in our legs and feet, until we had fallen silent, a little chiding, and then silent again, as we listened to the sound of our tread on the way.

People are kind to us. At night we were invited to sleep in a barn, our new dormitory with its friary of donkeys and convent of hens. I was asked by Brother Andrew if I understood their language.

Yes, I told him, they are saying, Please do not eat me. If you spare my life, I will lay you a very fine egg in the morning.

And he looked in wonder at the hens and thanked God for the wisdom that can penetrate mysteries, and Brother Bernard grunted, and I might easily suppose that he is the one who can speak the languages of the animals.

We slept on rough straw and as I fell asleep I felt, for the first time, the desire to be back in the friary where life is understood and I am under the shelter of my Master.

We were woken by a child who had been sent to bring us bread and milk, which was still warm from the sheep. The first taste of the milk was the strongest and the fullest, as if our appetites had shrunk to the shape of their first satisfaction. Rain and sunshine dripped through holes in the roof. Brother Andrew was smiling as he led us through the prayers. You O Lord will open my mouth. And my mouth shall declare your praise.

Our feet were aching to return to the journey. Bernard gathers his load, Andrew laid some stones into the sign of the cross. We stopped for breakfast and then Brother Bernard and I became impatient with Brother Andrew because he took so long to finish his food.

When we stopped again, in the shade of a tree, by the side of a river, stretching our legs, resting our tired, beaten feet, after we had performed our prayers, Brother Bernard and I ate the food we had kept back from breakfast. The bread was stale, the milk was sour, but after the labour of our day's walking, each bite and sip contained whole worlds. My body strengthened with every mouthful. I felt I had discovered something here today, to do with size and magnitude. If I had filled myself as quickly as Brother Bernard was doing, then I would not taste or feel or perceive so much.

Brother Andrew was looking miserable. He confessed that he had consumed all his food at breakfast. I gave him half of the rest of what I had. Brother Bernard threw him a scrap of bread.

A rainbow is ahead of us, which is either an auspicious omen or a signal sent to direct us by Master Roger. I explained to Brothers Andrew and Bernard that there are five principal colours, black, blue, green, red, and white. Aristotle said that there are seven but you can arrive at that by subdividing blue and green into two halves of dark and light. I could hear my voice above the music of a songbird and how preferable that music was at this moment so I became silent.

We could hear the bird as we walked. Brother Andrew and I looked above our heads for the songbird but we could not see it in the trees, just heard its song. I looked around and saw Brother Bernard's lips shaped forward, the whistling coming from them. I had not thought he was capable of such game or skill.

We wear the brown robes of our Order and the insignia of two keys on our chests, to signify our pilgrimage to Rome. The orders of angels watch our process towards Canterbury.

• • •

I have committed two sins, close to blasphemy, on the short way we have come. I have found myself wishing we were not carrying my Master's Book and his device for the Pope and his packet that we are to open when we have abandoned hope or hope has abandoned us. I have even neglected to pick up treasure I saw in the woods. I made my companions stop. We must go back, I told them. Or at least we have to stop and you must wait for me. It was not hard to persuade them to drop themselves down in a glade in the forest.

I went back to where the treasure was, cut it away from the earth, put it in my bag, and made my laborious way back to where my companions were, or at least should have been. I halted, went farther on, then back the way I had come. The trees looked like giants who were mocking me before taking me prisoner, casting their nets of leaves. I searched for different paths through the trees in the event I had taken a wrong turn in my tiredness. I stopped, I renewed my search; I went this way, and that, and returned again to the place where I first thought to find my companions – who, revivified by their rest, leaped out laughing at me from behind the trees.

My companions question me about my Master. They ask what it is we do up in the tower. I may of course not tell them about the Book.

We study, he teaches, I learn. Sometime we sing.

Sing what?

Different songs. The shape of music reveals the hidden structures of many things. Music is the power of connection coupled with beauty.

You sing?

In line with Aristotle's teaching. Music also teaches the virtues, courage and modesty and the other dispositions.

Who is Aristotle?

A great teacher. Perhaps the greatest.

A Franciscan?

No. Not a Franciscan.

A Dominican then?

Not a Cistercian?!

Bernard shows a particular antipathy to Cistercians.

He is not attached to any order, I tell them.

It is my favourite time with my Master when we sing. He strokes his beard, his eyes shine, his voice is large, full and profound. In singing we reach a communion. When singing he permits himself to be playful. He delivers a line, speaking of the earth, I answer him with the sky and stars, he repeats his, with more urgency, I hold fast, denying him his mud and earth; and then his voice rises higher lifting us both into a godly integration.

When I first was raised from the village into the friary, my Master told me stories. These were legends of the saints and fables concerning the beasts, the cunning of the fox, the lonely hunger of the lion, the foolishness of the donkey. Mistakenly, this is how I thought life would proceed, my Master and I sitting in the room at the top of the tower, the other pupils ignored. It was as if he was narrating these tales purely for me, in his deep voice, animated by the characters of the beasts into tones of excitement and anguish and wisdom. In this manner, I learned Latin. Later, I would be set the work of rewriting the fables in my own words, in different concisions. The fable of the frog and the mouse in five hundred words, one hundred, in fifty, in twenty. And, despite my Master, the matter was transmuted, from the stuff of marvel and wonder into a schoolroom task.

• • •

Saint Augustine's Day

After the trouble in Rochester, it was a relief to be back on the road. Our spirits soared, hills and clouds, sunshine. Our paces grew longer, Brothers Andrew and Bernard whistled the melody of the songbirds. As the days have proceeded, our bodies strengthen, the way is not so hard, our load not so heavy. This morning I had to tally the contents of the bags I was carrying in case I had left something behind, leaves of my Master's Book scattered in the road. We cover the ground with less complaint, with lightness.

Rays emanate in all directions from every point in the cosmos, conveying the force of things to proximous objects. The act of looking is a reciprocal exchange of powers with the object being looked at. The act of looking is all one and multifarious, radiation of heat, the influence of the stars, the efficacy of prayer.

Were it not that sin makes the body opaque, the soul would be able to perceive directly the blaze of divine love.

But there are still those difficult nights, a long day's walking behind us, the extra difficulty of climbing a hill to a town, which had seemed so close from the path, and finally permitted through the gates, but not to a bed – the bishop's men bar us here, the Cathedral chaptermen bar us there, neither group has a tolerance for Minorites. The forest seems preferable to this, lying together in a bed of moss and leaves; until someone takes pity, a pure heart who has no taste for the chaptermen or the bishop, to whom we companions represent, perhaps falsely, a purer way.

We wear the badge of the two keys to signify our ascent to Rome. There are other pilgrims on our way, some with the badge of the cross for their journey to the Holy Land, others with the shell for Santiago de Compostela. We climbed the hill towards Canterbury. Brother Andrew desired to sleep out in the open again, I suggested we find the Franciscan hospice, Brother Bernard said that we must visit the Cathedral first, shrive our sins at the shrine of Saint Thomas.

But first we must get through this, Brother Andrew said pointing ahead at the crest of the hill, where a throng was filling the road.

Two men in red jerkins were blocking the road with staves. A smaller man also in red was moving at the front of the waiting people. The men with staves had the heaviness and placidity of oxen whereas this one showed the narrow face and sudden movements of a quick river animal.

Brother Andrew tried to see over the heads.

What are they after? he asked me.

I do not know, I said.

Money, said Brother Bernard.

We watched the ox-men raise their staves and let a merchant pass in exchange for a coin that went into the scrip of the narrow man.

My hand went, as if in sympathy, to the clasp of my own scrip, in which I carry the Great Work.

It is a mockery that they use the bag of the pilgrim for profit, Brother Bernard said.

Brother Andrew and I looked at each other in wonder, partly because of his tone of indignation and partly too because this was the longest speech that either of us had ever heard him make.

Some of the pilgrims in the throng had moved away to stand at the side of the road so that they could beg the toll from others. Brother Bernard thrust a way through for us to stand at the front. A family had just been permitted past without any exchange of money.

A penny for strangers, a half-penny for pilgrims. Locals do not have to pay the toll.

This was told to us by a woman who carried a basket of fish. Have a fish, she said offering one to Brother Andrew. Because of your fairness, she said. Brother Andrew reddened, looked down to the ground. When you eat my fish you can say a prayer for me, she said.

We have no money, I told the man with the scrip.

He ignored me, held out his hand for a penny for the toll from the woman with the fish.

We go as pilgrims and strangers in the world, I said.

Then that should be a penny and a half for each of you, he said talking out of the side of his mouth. The rest of his body was still, just his eyes always in motion.

We serve God in poverty and humility. We do not use money.

Everyone knows how you friars live. God does not need your riches or your greed, the man said.

The conversation seemed to gladden him, as if it gave him the opportunity to display his wit. Many gave loud assent to his words and I marvelled at and feared this godless, upside-down place where pilgrims are exacted a toll to visit a shrine and the best men of learning and devotion are seen as exemplars of vice.

What is in your bag? the man said. Treasures, I expect.

None that you would recognise, I said.

We will not pay, Brother Bernard said.

Then you will not pass, the man said.

Brother Bernard lifted the man away from the ground as if he was shaking a fallen leaf, and coins rolled out of his scrip, and the throng at first did not know how to respond to this turn of events. But when Brother Bernard had hurled the man into one of the guards with the staves, and was already moving to the other, who hesitated, as if he could not decide whether to set upon him or flee, members of the crowd were scratching around on the ground for the fallen coins, and Brother Bernard was advancing upon the second guard, who made his decision, to flee, and we watched him run, and then Brother Bernard said, in his usual tone of plain announcement,

We should go on.

We went on.

In Rule Three of our Order, the blessed Saint Francis counsels, admonishes and begs his brothers that when we travel about the world, we should not be disputatious, contend with words, or criticise others, but rather should be gentle, peaceful and unassuming, courteous and humble, speaking respectfully to all as is due. Behold, he says, I send you as a sheep in the midst of wolves. Be therefore wise as serpents and as simple as doves.

Of the three of us, only Brother Andrew's behaviour in the matter of the toll men was without sin. The Cathedral rose above us, as we made our slow process towards it through elbows and shoulders of pilgrims, and Brother Bernard denied that he had behaved improperly.

It was right, he said.

When Brother Bernard takes a position he is unyielding.

Those men were demons, he said.

We must give greater penance, I said.

You do as your conscience tells you and I shall do likewise, he said.

I had not been prepared for such multitudes. Brother Andrew thrust himself for safety between me and Brother

Bernard. We were the sick, we were lepers and cripples, madmen, peasants, noblemen, pilgrims, all come to visit the relics of the saint. Beggars outside, preaching monks, merchants selling badges of the shrine.

Guard your bags, said a kindly-looking man on my left.

I carry three bags across my shoulders. In one are the necessities for my journey. In the second is space for the treasures I am to gather along the way, and the package my Master gave me that is only to be opened when we meet despair. The third bag is the scrip in which I carry my Master's Great Work. Alerted by the kindly man's warning, my hand went immediately to the third bag. I felt no stranger's hand, the seal was untouched.

There are cutpurses everywhere, the kindly man said.

He was not a monk, and nor was he a nobleman, because his costume was ragged and worn. He looked like someone who worked on the land, but a labourer on the land would not have spoken in Latin. His tunic was extraordinary: on the worn thread were pinned dozens of lead badges in the shape of saints and stars.

Even here?

Especially here. You have not been to Canterbury before?

We have been to nowhere before.

They call me Simeon the Palmer.

I am John the Pupil. My companions are Brother Bernard and Brother Andrew.

You are making penance?

This was the first encounter I had had on my journey in which I felt greeted with tenderness. There was something about Simeon the Palmer, his wise eyes, the steadiness of his hand on my arm, his odour of violets, that made me yearn to tell him about my childhood and my father's goats and life in the friary and my loneliness and my learning, and my mission and my Master, so that he should know to love him as much as I do.

We are making pilgrimage.

As am I. I go to Rome and then Compostela and on to the Holy Land.

You must carry a heavy burden of sins.

Most of them are not my own.

As we processed to the Cathedral gate, Simeon the Palmer explained to me that his occupation is to make pilgrimage on behalf of men who have a weight of sins, the desire to expiate them, and the money to pay someone else to do so on their behalf.

You make the pilgrimage and you perform the penance and your hirer stays at home and the consequence is that he is shrived?

That is how it works.

The world is a strange place.

Simeon the Palmer offered to make penance for us. You could divest your load on to me, he said.

I had not been prepared for the magnificence of the Cathedral, the glory of it, its size, the frescoes on the walls, the holy blaze of the windows. Brother Andrew and I made confession and washed our hands and the three of us were directed towards the foot of the stairs up to the martyr's shrine, where we removed our shoes and joined the procession of those who have been afflicted, by deformity or disease or riches, because we are all equal in sin.

We kissed the floor, we climbed the stairs on our hands and knees. A registrar sat with a book of miracles beside the shrine. Two Cathedral monks stood watch over the pile of jewels and money left by previous penitents. We had nothing to offer except our devotion and humility. Master Roger warns that men devoting themselves to holiness must try to avoid the short direct rays emanating from delectable things, such as women and food and riches. Prostrate at the martyr's shrine, I thought I detected an avaricious shine in Brother Bernard's eyes, a hungry vacuity mirroring the glistening of the jewels.

After we climbed back down and reclaimed our shoes and received the blessing for our pilgrimage, we were outside the Cathedral gate again and Simeon the Palmer was with us, pinning a new badge on to his tunic.

Paradise knocks on your door, a beggar said holding out his hand towards us, but seeing the look in Brother Bernard's eyes he quickly withdrew it again and turned his attention to other pilgrims.

My Master has placed a lonely burden on me. My companions believe that this is a pilgrimage of penance, so that is what it will have to be, for sins of pride and avarice and concupiscence. They do not know the purpose of our journey.

Saint Germanus's Day

Germanus began every meal by swallowing ashes. He never ate wheat or vegetables, drank no wine and did not flavour his food with salt. Germanus gave all his wealth away to the poor, lived with his wife as brother and sister, and for thirty years subjected his body to the strictest austerity. He spread ashes on his bed, whose only covering was a hair shirt and a sack. Such was his life that if there had not been any ensuing miracles, and there were many miracles, his holiness alone would have admitted him to the order of the saints.

•

I related the life and miracles of Saint Germanus and we stood by the boats at Dover with hands outstretched. Paradise knocks on your door, Brother Bernard said. Brother Andrew is not yet used to mendicancy. He was shy, his eyes downcast, his cheeks reddening. All the same, it was he who received the greatest alms. A pious captain gave us passage on his boat, in exchange for our consenting to lead a service after the boat had got under way, and a promise not to impede or obstruct or beg from the passengers and crew.

Brother Andrew stood on the prow as we waited for the boat to take to sea. Brother Bernard, who shows an aversion to water, sat in the stern wrapped inside his cloak. Brother Andrew and I watched the passengers climb on board, the pilgrims and merchants, and a great lord, whose passage demanded a retinue of servants and the transport of a score of horses, and carts overlaid with barehide, their wheels bound with iron, and boxes made of iron and wood, and barrels of wood, and bags made of leather and canvas.

The lord's chamberlain oversaw the loading of his master's goods. He was a man of powerful build, who roared out orders to his underlings who followed his instructions as if on pains for their lives.

They are like soldiers obeying their general, I said to Brother Bernard, trying to rouse him from his dolour.

When did you ever see a soldier? Brother Bernard said.

It is true. I have never seen a soldier, or a lion, or a feast on a great man's table, or a demon or an angel or a nun or a unicorn or a bride or a Jew. But before I set out on this journey I had never seen a cathedral or a man who made a living expiating other men's sins, and neither had I seen a great lord. This one was a man of small stature and sharp visage. He watched his chamberlain issuing the orders and drank from a small flask.

Maybe it was this, the possibility of all things now that I am upon this journey, or maybe it was the sight of Brother Andrew stretched forward on the prow, his arms fully extended, his body leaning into the breeze, or maybe it was the gentle motion of the boat rocking beneath me, that I felt touched by something forgotten from long ago, and was suddenly lifted, exhilarated, incorporeal, yet alive with the acuity of my senses.

The faces of the sailors are marked. One has a scar on his forehead, another is missing part of an ear. My Master, I would question you about this. Is beauty a signifier of virtue? These sailors may have been beautiful once. Does that mean they were once less vicious than today? Is Brother Andrew more virtuous than Brother Bernard, simply because the beauty of his face marks him out as being derived from, or at least compatible with, the angels? Were the sailors more virtuous when they were young, unmarked by experience and difficulty? We are born fallen. An unbaptised baby is not innocent. I would like to ask my Master if it is a blasphemy to think that the sailors are lifted by their travails, if there is an equation between the scars on their bodies and the godliness of their souls, if appearance is the converse of substance, not its mirroring cloak.

As it is written in Ezekiel, You are the seal of the image of God, full of wisdom and perfect in beauty. You have been in Eden, the garden of God; every precious stone was your covering.

On the aft part of the boat, the great lord's priest held a service for his lord and his retinue. Here, below, it was my office to lead the hymns and prayers of vespers.

Come O Holy Ghost, replenish the hearts of the faithful and kindle in them the fire of your love. We beseech you O Lord, that the virtue of the Holy Spirit may be present unto us: the which may mildly both purge our hearts, and also defend us from all adversities, through Our Lord Jesus Christ your Son: Who lives and reigns, God, with you, in the unity of the Holy Ghost, world without end.

We were the only three in orders taking passage on the boat, and Brother Andrew is too shy, Brother Bernard too rough, so I was given the office. My voice was fragile. I am unused to being the focus for so many other people's attention. I am not a priest nor had ever hoped to be. I could hear my own voice cracked and light. As I spoke the sacred words of prayer, I shut my eyes, imagined myself back in Master Roger's room, to give my voice, and heart, some strength.

Amen.

Let the mercies of the Lord give glory to him: and his wonderful works to the children of men. And let them sacrifice the sacrifice of praise, and declare his words with joy. They that go down the sea in ships doing work in the great waters, these have seen the works of the Lord, and his wonders in the deep.

Amen.

Simeon the Palmer brought himself towards me from out of the congregation of sailors. He complimented my sureness and my voice. He told me I spoke very well and assured me that the angels would smile upon our journey.

Brother Bernard is not enjoying the crossing. He sits with his head towards his knees, hugging himself as if desperate for the consolation of mother-love.

· · ·

The tumult on the harbour, the wonder of a different land, almost like ours, almost familiar, but so new and strange and barely known. We took such timid half-steps on land, as if expecting, after the solid earth of England, succeeded by the liquid of the crossing, that France should be composed of vapour. Brother Bernard does not understand French; I see this place through his eyes, as if the day has been slightly turned. The butcher wears a different hat.

As it says in my Master's Book, We expect things to be different in different places: manners and intellectual interests vary according to the diversity of regions; the body is altered by the heavens and when the body is changed the mind is aroused.

Brother Bernard stays close to me. Brother Andrew has to be admonished to remain with us, his attention is scattered upon the sights and sounds and smells of the harbour.

Here, I tell him, it is your turn to be the donkey.

Our load will tether him to the earth. We already carry too much. Our spoons and knives and bowls, my Master's Book in its shining sealed box, the apparatus for demonstration to the Pope, our breviary, the secret thing in its humble container that we may not open. According to the rule of our Order, we are not meant to carry bags; each of us carries two.

It is not hard to find our way. Pilgrims, jabbering, creeping, praying, mark the way in a slow penitential caravan. Until, suddenly, we are driven into the mud at the side of the road by the train of the great lord, riding four abreast on black chargers. His carts and oxen fill the road, as we try to restore order to our garments and our possessions. The seal on the box is unbroken. The apparatus is intact. My bag for the collection of treasures was emptied and I had to gather them from the road, combined with mud.

Brother Bernard hurled clots of mud at the oxen and the lord's servants, while I gathered my writing implements. I had thought I had chosen him for his strength and protection. Perhaps it was his soul I was concerned for, its safety, rather than that of my Master's treasures or my body. I smoothed out my scraps of parchment, wiped off as much of the mud as I could with the sleeve of my cloak. I write this through the dirt of the road.

Saint Hubert's Day

Hubert was a beautiful and courteous youth, noble-born, loved by all, whose single passion was for the hunt. On a Good Friday morning, when the virtuous were all inside church, Hubert was giving chase to a magnificent stag. The animal turned, and Hubert was stupefied to see a silver crucifix between its antlers, while at the same time a voice spoke these words, Hubert! Unless you turn to the Lord and lead a holy life, you will go quickly down to hell.

Hubert gave all of his wealth away, entered holy orders, and for the rest of his life, he was diligent in fasting and prayer, became famed for the eloquence of his sermons, was a friend to the poor and a scourge of idolaters, whom he sought out with the same passion that once he had brought to his love of the chase.

Our first night in Gaul, a night spent on the straw of a pilgrims' hospice, the snoring and dreams of the sleepers, the straw beneath us never still, rustling and shaking with the movements of mice, while the sleepers scratched at the fleas and lice that assailed them like an army besieging a town.

This is purgatory, Brother Bernard said shielding his eyes against the sunlight.

That is heresy, Brother Andrew said.

My throat and head were sore. I longed for my own bed, a less foul air, for a ministering remedy prepared by Master Roger.

In the men around us it was hard to identify God's pilgrims. The only sin that did not seem illustrated was the one of Pride.

Our goods were safe. I untied the rope that bundled them together. Some of the pilgrims were sleeping. Others were praying. Two men scourged themselves in the foulest corner of the room.

We recited matins on the road. And our hearts lifted as we sang,

> Blessed is the man who hath not walked in the counsel of the
> ungodly
> Nor stood in the way of the sinners
> Nor sat in the chair of pestilence.
> But his will is in the law of the Lord
> And on His law shall he meditate day and night
> And he shall be like a tree which is planted near running
> waters.

Around us, God's creation, the fields and trees, the birds, the stream we drink from. Let the friars take care not to appear gloomy and sad like hypocrites, but let them be jovial and merry, showing that they rejoice in the Lord, and becomingly courteous.

More things have gone into my bag of treasure, which, if God decrees this journey prosperous, I hope to return to

Master Roger full to overflowing, the bounty and reward for my Master's trust in me.

. . .

Fires on the hillside at night, the lodging ground of a company of vagabonds and pilgrims, an unnatural band of wolves and sheep, who stare at us as we approach.

Brother Andrew had no desire to proceed. Brother Bernard drove him on, we climbed the slope towards the fire. And as we approached, we heard a clinking, the dull repeating sound of his process, Simeon the Palmer amongst us.

Light flickered on the faces around us, as Simeon the Palmer in his noisy costume acted the host in this fairy supper.

You have eaten? You have food? I know, God will provide, and He has, His ways are many, and always marvellous, it is His work to look after His servants, a Father's strength, a Mother's care, sit with us, you will eat with us.

Mindful of Brother Bernard's suspicions (but he is always suspicious, he would interrogate the motives of an angel), I said that first we would need to make our own ground for the night. I have not yet collected many treasures for my Master, but the bag is not empty, and the work is a sacred one. And there is the bag with the Book, and there is the bag with the parts of the model for demonstration, and the secret package, for when hope is abandoned, and all of these I must keep secure. If I had just one bag to save, it would be easy to decide which it would be. The model is the fruit of our labour and study, but it is merely a thing, the Book is pure Thought, containing the wisdom of all times.

I looked for a place to lay our goods, I looked for a

place that was a soft place to be, a leafy bed between trees, free of slope or stones, where I might cover our precious things with soft earth, a landfall of fruit, a canopy of leaves and twigs. And I looked for a place where the eyes of the vagabonds would not follow me. The place was not to be found.

You are very modest, Simeon the Palmer said mistaking the nature of my precautions. We are all men, which is the same as saying that we are all God's creatures. There is a ditch away from the fire where we perform our necessary acts. No shame is attendant upon them.

Even for a friar, said a raggedy fellow sitting near the fire.

I left my bags with Brothers Bernard and Andrew (eyes downcast, skin reddened by the fire, the very image of the modesty that I was being accused of) who were already sitting by the fire with their expectant bowls. I walked down to the ditch, where I lifted my cloak and, unable to perform the act of voiding (my belly too empty, so many eyes upon me), waited in that position until I judged sufficient time had passed.

Sit with us, brother, Simeon the Palmer said. Tell us about your journey. Did you ride?

We are not meant to ride. Our Order forbids it.

Our redeemer rode on a donkey. Are you saying you are better than He?

The Palmer was in high spirits, joking, drinking, ladling soup into my bowl. He asked me what had brought us to our pilgrimage, but while I was still composing my answer, he pointed out men around us – that one had a vexatious wife, that one a smoking fireplace, that one a leaking roof, another had become a monk to avoid the punishment of the civil law.

And you? Brother Bernard said. When you make penance for your clients, do you repent your own sins?

I am the lamb, Simeon said. Chaste and clean. But you, you carry so much. I thought members of your Order went unburdened. Some bread? Have some bread. It is fresh.

He leaned towards me, and as he handed me a piece of bread, he whispered,

Hard to believe that you three are ordinary pilgrims.

I had no reply. I stuffed the bread into my mouth and chewed.

If you are in trouble, I can help. I have travelled this way many times. Where are you going?

As if helpless with the food in my mouth, I chewed.

Are there men in pursuit after you? Do you carry relics of the saints? Or maybe you are transporting monastery treasures that someone might mistakenly think you have no right to?

I finished the bread. No, I said, it is nothing like that.

He patted my arm, like a brother.

Of course not, he said.

When we were lying upon the ground, after Brother Andrew had preached – and it was marvellous to see, the softening of the rough company before Brother Andrew's beauty and God's truth – and after we had prayed and we were waiting for sleep, with its nocturnal temptations, to take us, and the world was so loud around us, louder than the hospice, because this time there were dark birds in the branches of trees, the rustle of beasts in the woods, I grew afraid.

I gathered up our bags and I woke Brother Andrew and Brother Bernard and told them we must go, silently and in haste, and they were sleepy and reluctant but I drove them on, like a shepherd with his small flock, and we made our way out of the lodging ground, and there were eyes upon us, cold in the firelight, watching our departure, and there was a clinking of metal that might have belonged to Simeon the Palmer.

I was not able to explain my fear to my companions. We set forth along the dark path. We slept finally, at dawning, in a chapel on a hill.

We woke hungry, it was so late in the day. Sun shone through the windows, our Saviour born, the kings from the east bearing him gifts. We said matins, even though the hour was so late.

Outside, we gave thanks for God's creation. The earth was wet from an early-morning rainfall. I taught my companions a song that I used to sing with Master Roger. Brother Bernard, into whose head learning could never stick, immediately learned the words and the rhythm. We sang until our throats were dry, and then we drank from a stream and sang some more until, I think it was Brother Andrew who began it, we replaced our music with laughter. Laughter is a gift of the Holy Spirit. The Devil is powerless against it.

We laughed, without object or cessation. We laughed without ever, it seemed, being able to imagine a time without laughter, a moment when the world did not consist of the three of us lying on the grass outside a chapel in France, beating the damp grass with our fists.

Until we saw the men climbing the hill towards us. They were wet, cloaks and habits heavy from their night out in the rain, which was maybe why we had not heard them approach. Simeon the Palmer's badges hardly made a sound as he walked.

But he was cheerful, as ever. He showed joy at seeing us. He praised our sharpness in finding a dry place to pass the night.

And your goods? I see you look after them. You are careful stewards of your treasures. Not a drop of rain upon them.

The men's faces were stern. They came into the chapel and they gathered around our packages and I made to stop them, I thrust through them and reached for the shining box in which my Master's Great Work is contained, but there were too many of them and only one of me, and the men seized me, held my arms tight, helpless, by my side. I looked to Brother Bernard and Brother Andrew but Brother Andrew was gone and five of them, maybe six, were subduing Brother Bernard, a confusion of cloaks and arms that might have been an occasion for mirth if it had not been for the enormity of what was taking place, our powerlessness, our despair, our fall, we had come this way and we had hardly begun our journey and already it was over.

We will take this, call it a shelter tax. We slept in the wet, you were in the dry.

There was nothing I could do against them. Simeon the Palmer took two of the bags, the box, shook it slightly, held it up to his ear.

You can go, he said. Take the rest of your goods with you. It is just a tax, we are not robbers.

I fought. I shouted, We have letters of credential from the Pope!

Or we can go. You can stay here. We will leave you to your chapel. The rain has stopped.

They tied my arms behind my back. They did the same to Brother Bernard, although that process took longer and required more assailants to keep him still. Helpless, we watched them leave. I wept.

And through the entrance of the chapel, where the Last Judgement was painted on the walls around the doorway, came Brother Andrew, creeping, carrying two of our bags. He unfastened the bonds that tied us.

I prayed for guidance and Brother Andrew joined in and Brother Bernard watched me.

And now? Brother Bernard said.

We follow them. We retrieve the box. Somehow.

As we gathered up our things, Brother Bernard blamed Brother Andrew for fleeing from the fight. I told him that if he had not, all three of us would be in bondage in God's house. I carried the bag that Brother Andrew had saved in which were the parts for the model to demonstrate to the Pope. Brother Bernard carried a bag that contained Brother Andrew's bowl and spoon and our breviary. The rest of our goods were with the band of thieves.

We made our way down from the chapel towards the foot of the hill. We could hear the men shouting ahead of us as they walked.

It had fallen upon me to be the leader of our little party. I am not quite sure how it happened; I am the youngest; I am the only one not in holy orders. I am a pupil, not a friar. Maybe it was because I knew more than they did: I knew the purpose of our journey.

Why do we have letters from the Pope? Brother Bernard asked me.

To speed us on our way. The box is for him.

What is in the box? Brother Andrew said.

The whole world, I told him.

Hard to believe that something so small could contain the whole world, Brother Bernard said in his usual tone of moody scorn.

I did not explain. I was preparing myself for the battle ahead. I would, I decided, fight for the Book with my life, if that was what it would cost. My Master's Great Work ends with a ferocious self-humbling and an awkward politics, flattering the Pope, exalting him as one who should be worshipped, the vicar of the church, as God on earth; but, before that, it is a promise of knowledge that will shake creation, as Aristotle instructed Alexander. Master Roger will be Clement's Aristotle, his indispensable tutor, counsellor, father.

And there are novelties in there, the secrets of magnetism and an ever-burning lamp, or how to make a firecracker to amuse children, the powder that is antidote to the most deadly snake bite, the slaying of poisonous things with the lightest touch. How to make an instrument of a year-old hazel twig that will vibrate to the natural powers of the earth. These things are offered to the Pope, not to a knave and his band.

It is the world, I told them, in a book.

A bible?

Almost as important.

It was a heresy for them to presume to take it, and an awful danger too, that they might read of the consuming fire that no water can put out, or of how to manufacture the crack louder than thunder that Gideon employed to defeat the Midianites.

The vicious company was stopping. We stopped behind the shelter of three trees. They were in a rough circle near a roadside altar beneath which twigs and leaves had been laid for pilgrims to make a votive fire.

We are higher up than they, and we have the advantage of suddenness, Brother Bernard said.

An advantage that would quickly turn to its reverse if we have nothing to support it with.

We have the sun at our backs, Brother Andrew said. Maybe they will be blinded as we ambush.

It was clear that he did not have the capacity for a fight and I could hardly blame him, but guilt at his earlier desertion was driving him to affect an appetite for battle.

I looked at the might of our tiny army. I examined our armoury. I made as if Master Roger was with us, to counsel us, to general our legions. And I asked Brother Andrew to repeat what he had said, and he did, and the spirit of God directed me.

Phaeton and his chariot will help us, I said.

I got to my knees to open the bag that contained the apparatus for the model to demonstrate to the Pope.

What are they doing? I asked.

What are you doing? Brother Bernard said. Praying?

Just tell me what they are doing.

They are standing, maybe they are disputing, Brother Andrew said.

One is reaching for the box but Simeon will not let him have it, Brother Bernard said.

Do not let them open the box, I said.

I had thought that constructing the apparatus under the scrutiny of my Master would prepare me for the work of assembling it at any occasion. My Master's eyes are stern and steady, the faculty for being observed is most acute under his scrutiny. But here, on the side of the hill, our most precious work the possession of a company of unworthy thieves, my hands were shaking, my fingers fumbling, my skin pricking with labour and fear, the metal support legs fell on to their sides, like a giant insect falling dead to the earth.

Some of the other men seem to be grasping for the box too, Brother Andrew said.

And a smaller number are shoving against them. They are arguing, Brother Bernard said – but how are we going to stop them?

I do not know. Think of something. Sing. Dance.

The Palmer is shaking his head, Brother Andrew said.

He's losing the argument, Brother Bernard said.

One of them is putting on your cloak, Brother Andrew said.

Maybe, I feared, my Master was wrong and the villagers were right, and his powers had nothing to do with investigation and repetition; and at my touch, no power would assist me.

They are about to open the box, Brother Bernard said.

Were it not for the apple! Brother Andrew sang walking lightly down the hill towards the robbers.

We should not have been saved! Brother Bernard sang walking more quickly to catch up with him.

Were it not for the bondage! sang Brother Andrew.

We would still have been slaves! sang Brother Bernard.

I could see the unworthy band now, as my apparatus was constructed, its foreleg embedded in the earth. I was fixing the lens into place now. But one of the hind legs kept folding at its mid-joint, like a goat with a broken knee.

The next two lines, they sang together:

If not for captivity!

We would never be free!

And then Brother Bernard performed a little dance, moving as I have seen my father and the village people do at feast times, kicking his legs to and fro with his arms crossed over his chest. And Simeon the Palmer looked stupefied, but some of his men were laughing; and for a moment the box, which is shining and closed with a seal, and engraved for the Pope, was forgotten in a disputant's hand, his knife halted in the air, and I had aimed the lens and it had caught the sun, and Phaeton's chariot was riding through the glass to the patch of tinder beneath the altar. And I did pray then. I prayed to God Almighty and to the Virgin and to the Holy Spirit and to Christ our Redeemer, and to the orders of angels, and Brother Bernard was dancing and the men were watching him, and the sun shone through my Master's lens and the wood that I was aiming at received the chariot. But it did not catch alight. A humble circle of light held steady beneath the altar, and the company was tiring of Brother Bernard's show, and just as I was beginning to open myself up to the sin of despair, a raindrop from the leaves of the tree above me, or it might have been an angel's tear, fell onto the centre of the glass, and the sun, magnified further, lit the first spark; and the fire caught and licked and jumped, and the robbers stared away from Brother Bernard, who was still dancing, and they gazed in fright upon the fire beneath the altar, before they fled, leaving our goods scattered behind.

In such a way did we effect our first escape from Simeon the Palmer.

. . .

Once there was a frog who lived in the woods who was befriended by a certain mouse. In front of them was a pond, which the mouse wished to cross but had not the means of doing so. The frog said to the mouse, Trust me, friend mouse, we will tie one of your legs to one of mine with this string, and in this way, we will cross the pond together. The mouse was very afraid, for any body of water was a matter for dread and fear for him, but he trusted his friend and he had witnessed the strength of his swimming; so the frog tied their legs together and in this way, despite several submersions beneath the water for the anxious mouse, they crossed the pond in safety. Whereupon a great hawk swooped down upon them and carried them both away.

· · ·

Saint Boniface's Day

The beloved founder of our Order instructs us to preach as we travel. Our sermons begin with an account from the lives of the saints. In this way, just as the faith of the sinner Saint Boniface was inflamed by the suffering of the martyrs, we light a fire in the imagination of our listeners that ignites an apprehension of the glory of God and the beauty of His Creation.

But Brother Bernard is not a good preacher. In Latin, even in English, he is halting and raw. When he attempts French, he is stuttering, hesitant, unmanned. Brother Andrew is almost equally shy, but his beauty attracts the largest numbers and the greatest charity. Yesterday, we had to help Brother Bernard with words, even the Latin ones, because his audience was shrinking away, bringing dishonour on the speaker, on our Order, maybe even upon our Truth.

On the edge of a wood, by a dip of the river, we rested. I faced my companions as if they were an audience of simple villagers and I narrated the glory and martyrdom of Saint Boniface.

When Boniface, seeking salvation for his sins of lust and fornication, went to Tarsus, he saw the various kinds of torture devised by an impious executioner upon the gentle bodies of Christians. Aflame with the love of Christ, he called upon God and ran up to the martyrs and sat at their feet, kissing their chains and saying,

O struggling martyrs of Christ, trample on the Devil! The torments you are suffering for the love of God will soon be over. Then you will be clothed in the glory of immortality and enjoying the vision of your King. You will render him praises of heavenly song amidst the choirs of angels and you will see the wicked men who are torturing you now themselves being tortured in the abyss of eternal calamity!

Simplicius the judge heard all this and had Boniface brought before him. Who are you? he asked. Saint Boniface replied, I am a Christian and am called Boniface.

The judge in his anger ordered him to be hung up and his body to be slashed with hooks until the bones showed; then splinters of wood were driven under his fingernails. The blessed martyr of God looked up to heaven and eagerly bore his pains, and the impious judge, seeing this, ordered molten lead to be poured into his mouth. The holy martyr said, I give you thanks, Lord Jesus Christ, Son of the living God!

Then the judge ordered a tub to be brought and filled with boiling pitch, into which the holy martyr was plunged head first, but again he remained unharmed, so at the judge's command his head was cut off with a sword. The moment this was done, a tremendous earthquake shook the ground, and many of the heathens, perceiving the power of Christ through the body of the martyr, became believers.

Amen, said Brother Bernard.

Now you try, said Brother Andrew.

Brother Bernard looked at the trees ahead of him, at his toes lapped by the river, as if the dirt swirling away from his feet could be the picture of his salvation.

Bernard cleared his throat. He stood. He held his hands

together in front of him and then behind and then in front of him again. Finally he began, saying,

When Boniface the fornicator came to Tarsus, he saw the Christian martyrs undergoing terrible tortures – What kinds of tortures?

They might have been whipped or flayed, I said.

Or had burning coals heaped upon them, Brother Andrew said.

Which? Brother Bernard said.

They were whipped and flayed, I told him; and we instructed him to proceed.

Brother Bernard proceeded, saying,

He fell to his knees, he kissed their chains, his heart burst into fire.

Brother Andrew moved to correct him but stopped himself.

And Brother Bernard proceeded, saying,

Weeping Boniface ordered the martyrs to trample upon the Devil.

He stopped. Where was the Devil? he said.

We knew that Brother Bernard was asking this question to delay the remainder of his recitation, which doubtless he had forgotten, but we asked him to explain himself.

Where was the Devil? he said. Was he in the executioner or the judge or was he there standing by the sides of the martyrs mocking them?

Maybe in all those places, Brother Andrew said; and looked at me, because he respects my greater learning.

What does the Devil look like? Brother Bernard said.

The physical eye cannot see the Devil as he is, I said.

Why is that? Brother Bernard said. I have heard of those who have seen the Devil.

Because the Devil is spirit and it is the opinion of almost all the masters that only spirit can see spirit.

But, Brother Andrew said, angels are spirit too, and scripture tells us of the angels who visited Lot and the angels who descended to earth and engendered a race of giants from...

His natural modesty prevented him from finishing his sentence.

I quoted to my companions the words of the Apostle Paul, Our wrestling is not against flesh and blood, but against principalities and powers, against the rulers of this darkness, against the spirits of wickedness in high places.

The judge was the highest, so was the Devil in him? Brother Bernard said.

The Devil is in all the enemies of men, who try to steer the righteous away from Christ's path.

And who prey upon the righteous, Brother Andrew said.

So the Palmer. The Devil is in him.

Brother Bernard believes the Palmer to be the image of the Devil, and maybe he is right. Maybe the Devil is a slightly built man with a receding chin and dark eyes and dark hair that stands on end who smells of violets.

At least he is his ally, I said. The gospel of Matthew treats of the Devil, and that is the fifth book. Five is the apostate number, since if it is joined to any other odd number as a multiplier it always shows itself, perhaps at the beginning, certainly at the end. Thus the Devil, withdrawing from the foursquare of eternal stability, is the first to ally himself with wicked men, who are as unequal numbers, and shows himself in his iniquity, often at the beginning, and always at the end of act or speech. So it is written, and so we saw in the iniquity of Simeon the Palmer.

So how did Boniface trample on the Devil? Brother Bernard said.

He did not trample on the Devil, he was exhorting the martyrs to do so, Brother Andrew said.

By resisting the temptation to renounce their Saviour, by not succumbing to the injuries inflicted upon their bodies to prejudice their eternal souls, I said.

So where was he? Brother Bernard said. Saint Christopher saw the Devil, and marched beside him. And your Master told you to beware of demons who look like men and demons who look like women.

I was about to explain to Brother Bernard that a demon is different in kind from the Devil, but I did not, because, instead of looking for the words to do so, I was wondering how he could have known of a conversation that I had had alone with my Master. And so, although fearing their answer, I asked my companions this, to which Brother Bernard answered that he and Brother Andrew had read from my chronicle.

I do not know how they had the opportunity to read it. I would not have thought they had any more desire to read it than it had the desire to be read. These notes have no intended audience, except for my conscience and God, and the half-forgotten eyes of Master Roger.

Brother Andrew said, Why did you not write about the flowers we saw or the kind clerics of Laon? Why did you not write about the swim we had in the river, the touch of the water and the sunshine on our flesh?

And Brother Bernard said, Why did you not write about the men we saw, strapped together, marching to their deaths?

And Brother Andrew said... – but I was not listening.

Nor was I able to answer. It was as if I had been flayed and my bowels exposed, inspected, groped, found wanting. It was not the judgement that had been passed on me, it was the fact of the exposure that disturbed me so. What was internal had been made external. My companions had looked beneath my skin. And, further, they might have read descriptions I had made of them and my words were not always, particularly in the case of Brother Bernard, statements of praise.

They did not draw attention to my descriptions of them. These did not seem to be occasions for offence or dispute. They asked me about the purpose of our journey. And I explained to them that this had not been designed to be an expedition of penance but a journey to deliver something marvellous to the Vicar of Rome, and now that they knew we are not penitents, but messengers, what exercised them were not the various qualities of our burden, but the accounts I had not made, my persistence in seeing the world through different eyes.

When I looked through these shreds, I felt sure that some were missing, but I was unable to ask my companions about this.

We accepted a ride in a peasant's cart, because now that they are not penitents but messengers my companions are no longer concerned about breaking the Franciscan rule. The ox cart was slow, it might even have made slower progress than we could achieve on foot, but it was welcome to be sitting in a cart, legs swinging in the air, relieved of the burden of walking.

Franciscans do not carry. Franciscans do not ride in ox carts. This maybe was why we were greeted with such suspicion in the peasant's village. A mother crossed herself. Children ran from our approach. None of this assisted Brother Bernard in his preaching. No one heeded his words, which halted and stopped and the life and glorious martyrdom of Saint Boniface went unsaid. I heard a clinking in the distance, but I think it was the sound from a blacksmith's shop.

• • •

In addition to our customary fasts, we observe the Ember Day fasts, four times a year, following the four fallacious seasons.

There are many reasons for this practice. The first is that spring is warm and humid, summer hot and dry, autumn cool and dry, winter cold and wet. Therefore we fast in the spring to control the harmful liquor of voluptuousness in us; in summer, to allay the noxious heat of avarice; in autumn, to temper the aridity of pride; in winter, to overcome the coldness of malice and lack of faith.

We fast because the body of man consists of four elements, earth and water and air and fire; and the soul consists of three powers, the rational, the concupiscible, and the irascible. In order to control the elements and powers within us, we fast for three days four times a year.

We fast to atone each season for our faults in that season. Furthermore, we fast for three days to atone for the faults committed in each month; we fast on Wednesday because Judas betrayed Our Lord on that day, and on Friday because that is the day Christ was crucified.

Furthermore, we fast in spring to wither the seeds of the vices and protect the innocence of the child; we fast in autumn to offer to God the fruits of good works and to mature by righteousness. In winter when the grass dies, we fast because we die in this world but hope to grow in prudence and virtue. And in summer, as the sun beats upon us, as our feet swell and bleed, admonishing us of the ordeal of Our Lord and how we strive to emulate His last journey and will always fail, but in our failure reach closer to Him, as the branches that cross our path seem to love Brother Andrew the greatest, as all natural things do, and cut into his face and arms with a bloody kiss, we fast in Pentecost week, because the Holy Spirit comes in that time and we ought to be fervent in the Spirit.

We fast, and the people feast and dance. We preach, not for alms, but to share the joy of our teaching. Sore from our journey, we gathered to preach at the side of a market square. Brother Bernard affected reasons why he could not preach. His throat was sore, his mind confused. His tongue lay heavy and was unable to twist into the strange shapes of the French language. So he became the helper and respondent. Relieved that the burden of office was lifted from him, he was vigorous in his work. He ingratiated himself with those listening, making jokes, praising the beauty of children held in their mothers' arms.

Later, in the woods, trying to make our beds in the discomfort under the trees, we discussed why we had been driven out from the village. They had thrown stones at us, and we had suffered bruises and cuts and it was a miracle of God's grace that we escaped heavier injury. Brother Andrew said that the villagers were enemies of God, inspired by the Devil. Brother Bernard said that it was because they thought we were monks, like the Cistercians who preach chastity and practise incontinent concupiscence, but those were not the actual words he spoke: the epithets he used were borrowed from the tavern rather than church and he would not answer where he had found the words.

I thought, but I did not share this with my companions, that I had seen a member of Simeon the Palmer's band pointing in our direction and whispering to people in the village, and that he had maybe inspired the sudden violence that was hurled our way. I did not say this because I seem to see and hear evidence of Simeon the Palmer wherever we go, and the clinking that I was sure was proof of his impending malice turned out to be the scraping of branches together in the night wind.

Saint Edgar's Day

And England was sorely troubled by the Danes so that in many kings' days there could be no peace but a perpetual war. And the Danes prevailed against England and they brought it under their subjection, for their cruelty and tyranny were so great that, without sparing of anything, they burnt and destroyed.

But at the last it pleased Almighty God that this tyranny should cease, and He sent of His grace into the kingdom a peaceable king named Edgar, at whose birth angels sang that peace should be in his time, and so in his days there was no war in England.

We have been given such hospitality in this walled town that nearly all thoughts of the Palmer and his men have been banished.

We have been pampered, further than we merit or require, because a serving girl at a great house is displaying a love for Brother Andrew. He softens the hearts of all who see him. She brings him special fancies from her master's table and Brother Andrew is too kind to reject them. He did the first time, but her manner was so fallen, her spirit bruised, that he could not bring himself to do it a second time. She spreads a cloth for him in the courtyard, orders his bowl and spoon so daintily, just so.

She brings us food too, because Brother Andrew asks her to do so, but otherwise ignores us entirely. We do not exist for her, there is no room for us in her world, and maybe she is right, Brother Andrew's beauty is blazing, obliterating all else. And we are silent, we turn to our own bowls and spoons, we hardly dare to look up, and when we do, we look away, to the cathedral spire.

Beauty speaks to beauty. She takes him away from the courtyard, leads him up a staircase into an apartment built into the wall. The animals were gathered into the Ark two by two. The swan on the lake mourns the loss of his dame. The friar stands alone, and there seems to be a kind of terrible pride to this, lifting ourselves above nature to mimic the loneliness of Our Lord. How hard it must be to resist the Devil, when, like the beast in the field, he comes in the guise of what seems so natural.

When they return, and find us at prayer, her costume is disturbed. In her modesty or maybe shame, a reddening blooms between her breasts.

• • •

Brother Bernard grunted. He lives in a world where things, for good or ill, happen to other people. I think he would like the opportunity for sin; sometime I think that he hates Brother Andrew for his capacity to arouse the desires of others.

I try to console Brother Andrew. I say,

Blame not him who falls, but who remains fallen. It is man's lot to sin; it is the Devil's to remain in sin.

This does not console him. Brother Andrew beats himself as we walk towards Paris. In a kind of ecstasy he scourges himself for his sin.

As the Apostle Paul wrote to the Hebrews,

And almost all things, according to the law, are cleansed

with blood: and without shedding of blood there is no remission.

Brother Bernard helps a merchant by lifting his cart out of muddy ruts. He could carry either of us, lift us in the air with one arm, heave us like a sack of apples across his back, walk further up the hill as if unburdened.

But maybe I have eaten some of my Master's excess dignity along with his knowledge. I should not like to be lifted in the air like a sack of apples. I used to play, I am sure of that, but what is surprising to me is that I have no recollection of it.

And Brother Andrew may not be lifted in the air or otherwise aided on his journey. Brother Andrew is crawling this next stretch of road because Brother Andrew is making penance for having succumbed to temptation. Brother Andrew is crawling on his hands and knees, his brown cloak further browned from the mud of the road, reddened by the blood of his knees, so that it approximates, in a strange correspondence, to the colour of the leather covers of my Master's Book. Brother Andrew's face is streaked with mud and tears but his eyes shine, cheerful, pure. Flies murmur around him because all living things admire Brother Andrew.

Brother Andrew is beautiful. Brother Bernard is strong. I am merely clever.

• • •

Saint Ephrem's Day

Cain built the first city. At the suburbs of Paris, we rested, to prepare for Babylon. I thought I saw an eagle in the sky, like the portent that appeared to Philip of Macedonia on the birth of his son, but it was only a pigeon coming to rest on a rooftop.

Brother Andrew's feet are wounded from the journey. Brother Bernard was hungry. I shared both conditions, but I felt that I had to simulate perpetual good cheer, which, I was sorry to see, had become an irritation to my companions, even gentle Brother Andrew. Brother Andrew preached in the growing light, Brother Bernard and I collected alms and blessed the alms-givers. Resuming our journey, climbing to the city wall, permitted through the gate on account of our clerical garb, we went in discord.

Cain's work dazzled us. Cats and caged birds and stars. Towers and bells. All of life is here: lace workers, lepers, boatmen rowing under Le Petit Pont, merchants, scholars, artisans, rag pickers, grammarians, barbers, charcoal bearers.

The city is a labyrinth. We walked in circles, we repeated our steps, stumbling past a stable on our right hand in the afternoon that we had passed on our left hand in the morning. People looked at us with suspicion and doubt, refused to answer our questions, covered their faces, or feigned friendship in the manner of Simeon the Palmer and tried to deliver us into houses of gambling and drinking and sin. Finally we found it, the habitation of a former pupil of my Master, on a blood-spilled street of butchers and slaughterhouses, where students take lodgings above the shops.

We slept on the floor of my Master's former pupil, in the space he cleared for us amidst the clutter of parchment and glass.

When I awoke, I thought for a moment that I was back in my Master's room. Books and lenses directed at me their familiar species, the shapes and smells of the time before my journey. And at his table was my Master's former pupil, leaning over instruments, looking through lenses. My Master's eyes magnified merely reveal a greater sagacity. The eyes of his former pupil looked like two enormous grey fish swimming in a pale sea.

You have brought me something? he asked.

Just the greetings of Master Roger.

No instruments, no lenses, no letter?

No letter, no.

I do not know why it should have given me a satisfaction close to voluptuousness to deny the former pupil even a letter from my Master. His hands were cut with fresh scars. His body was composed of straight lines and angles.

Nothing?

Happily, I could confirm that this was so.

Brother Bernard farted. As if this was the cock crowing to start their morning, he stirred, as did Brother Andrew. Brother Andrew's eyes opened. He gathered his cloak around his body as if for protection, climbed into a kneeling position and silently prayed. Brother Bernard lay with his arms crossed, behind his head.

The former pupil ignored them both.

I will write to him nonetheless. You will deliver this quickly on your return.

We shall not be returning quite so quickly.

The scholar returned to his desk. He seemed to be jealous of any interruption to his work with lenses, my company; even a letter to my Master was little more than a nuisance separating him from his work of cutting and polishing and ordering. I am familiar with this work from my Master's room. If he had not spread his mind so far, from stars to blood, the outer world and the inner, his work on optics would have been so much more advanced than this.

What do you desire from me? the scholar said.

We should desire nothing from you, Brother Bernard said.

And the journey has been so long already and we have so much farther yet to go, and when we were walking through the streets last night, a dark suspicion took hold of me, that we were never to reach our destination, there are too many places to fall, my incapacities are too many that I should try to play general of this expedition. We are too imperfect, the world too inhospitable, we are destined to fail, the road is too hard, and all I had wished from the scholar was just a touch of welcome, an answering fellowship, a support and a rest. We share a mutual loyalty, or so I had thought. I had not expected his suspicion.

We will make our way, I said. Thank you for permitting us to stay the night.

So haughty, the scholar said. You are not pilgrims. You may not even be Franciscans. This baggage – did Christ carry so much as a breviary? He preached with the enthusiasm of his heart, unencumbered. What are you? Are you thieves? Have you come to steal from me? Show me what is in your bags.

I told him no. I told him they were not for him.

This is not Christian hospitality, I said. Wherever brothers meet one another, let them act like members of a common family.

You quote from the rules of our Order? Let me quote to you: The brothers should appropriate neither house, nor place, nor anything for themselves; and they should go confidently after alms, serving God in poverty and humility, as pilgrims and strangers in this world. Why do you carry so much? That bag that makes the sound of metal and glass, show it to me.

I was adamant. And, yes, haughtily, not in the true spirit of humility, I told him that we would deliver his letter to Master Roger upon our return, which we did not expect to be soon.

. . .

Not because my companions asked me to, but because my Master tells me to, I shall remember to be instructed by the world, to attend the evidence of my own senses, to remember that nothing is too humble to be the evidence of God's love.

Having left the scholar's apartment, feeling the irritation I was carrying at his rough manners towards us begin to diminish, we made our way towards the Holy Chapel to pay obeisance to and pray at the holy relic of Our Lord's Crown of Thorns. We had to shove through all manner of people.

Cain built the first city. He also devised weights and measures, those instruments of profit and usury which deny the sharing of God's abundance. Produce filled the air with its stench. Cathedral bells could hardly be heard above the merchants' cries making a great unholy song.

> Birds, pigeons, fish salted, fish fresh
> Good cress from Orleans
> I have chestnuts from Lombardy
> I have raisins from overseas
> I have the good cheese of Brie

The people shoved against us and moved us apart, and Brother Bernard was no longer with us. Near to a stall selling tripe, Brother Andrew stood, weighed down with his own bags as well as those of Brother Bernard.

I asked Brother Andrew where our companion was, and he replied that he had gone down an alley to answer a need. We waited together, giving the last of our food as alms to a passing leper who was tolling his sad little bell, but were driven away from the tripe stall by the press of customers. We went past a copyist who was cutting words into a page of vellum, towards a tavern into which lewd men went in and from which blasphemous song came out. By turns we looked for our missing brother at a water trough, a fruit seller, a dealer in birds, whose cages on high sticks contained creatures of prodigious colour and sound.

Leaving Brother Andrew with all our bags, I looked for the alley that Brother Bernard might have gone down. I returned to Brother Andrew, not having found our missing brother.

In our innocence, we speculated at what may have befallen Brother Bernard. He has the strength of three men, we could not imagine him waylaid, overpowered. And for what? He was carrying nothing. But he was gone.

Brother Andrew said,

Perhaps he has gone on to the Chapel. Maybe he is waiting for us to catch up with him.

So we gathered our bags and thrust our way through the street towards the chapel, but, after we had walked the distance towards it, a tall tower of light, there was no sign of Brother Bernard.

And Brother Andrew said,

Perhaps he is where he left us. He might still be waiting for us.

So we made our way back, and we returned finally to the merchant of birds, the tavern, the tripe stall. The day was hot, my body was sweating and sore under the weight I was carrying. This was not as when we had grown tired and vexatious on the road, at least then our labours had purpose. Here, we were vagabonds on a multitudinous street in the place that Cain built. And still there was no sign of Brother Bernard.

Perhaps he has returned to the house of the scholar, Brother Andrew said.

We could have returned there, we could have gone on again, to visit the Crown of Thorns; as we were making our deliberations, a woman gave Brother Andrew wine to drink. He told her he had no coins to pay for it. She told him she did not wish for coins from him; and by now we are wise in the world and could see what she might desire from him. He shared the drink with me and returned the flask to the woman and he thanked her and at no moment did he permit her eyes to match with his, and when their hands briefly touched as he was returning the flask I saw Brother Andrew's body shiver.

To the man behind the tripe stall, I described Brother Bernard, his cloak, his size, the colour of his hair, which is the most beautiful part of him, a golden brown. I asked if he had seen him. I said that an injury or calamity might have befallen him.

The man of the tripe stall, whose produce was the most foul-smelling of all in the street, seeming to contain the odours of the slaughterhouse as well as the farmyard, the fear of the animals as they died, laughed at me.

The calamity of Bacchus, he said. I saw that man leave the tavern in company of others. They are probably on their way to another.

Brother Bernard has fallen into bad company. We carry the bags he has abandoned.

We went from tavern to tavern, and each time we were directed on from another foul den where there was wreckage on the floor and bad temper in the tavern keeper's face. Brother Bernard's path was leading in the direction of the Holy Chapel, a profane passage towards the holiest of relics.

Finally we were again there, at the building of light that contained Christ's Own Crown. We had decided to resume the hunt after visiting the shrine. Brother Andrew delayed going in. He held his place, and penitents behind us complained at the delay to enter the Chapel door.

We will find our companion, I said.

I am not worthy, he said.

None of us is worthy, I said.

Each night I battle temptation, he said. And having succumbed once, the temptation is even greater.

Blame not him who falls, I said, but who remains fallen. And the woman with the flask. You were strong enough to resist temptation there. The Devil tempts only the very good and the very bad.

This did not console him. I fancied I saw the Crown ahead of us, in the light of the Chapel windows or maybe the windows were the receivers of light originating from the Crown, but then we were shoved aside by the penitents.

Brother Andrew's mouth muttered prayers. He interrupted them to whisper,

But I liked it. I would do it again.

We will return here after we find our brother, I said making my voice resolute. We will find him, and we will return here, and we will pray together, the three of us, and we will absolve our sins, and then we will resume our journey.

And we did find him, when we had all but given up hope of doing so, and we did resume our journey, but we did not pray before the Crown of Thorns, and the events did not transpire as we expected them to.

As I write this, my fingers are cramped from the pen, my head is bare to the wind, and I am hungry.

And it is hard not to see a portent in this: we never did pray at the Crown of Thorns; we may never reach journey's end.

. . .

In the tavern where we came at last to our straying brother, the maids were dressed in filthy clothes that revealed squares and triangles of flesh, a geometry of sin, and their flesh looked dark and bruised in the struggling light.

Brother Bernard had fallen in with a company of dissolute clerics, found his place among them with their love of wine and disputation and song. Brother Bernard was beating out a rhythm on the tavern table, his weak head for learning the liturgy belied by his capacity to memorise the words of their drinking songs, his powerful voice bellowing out the chorus, *I suffer much, Both day and night! Oh, Why are you telling me to sing?!* And there was a delight in his eyes, a foolish happiness on his face that is normally so immobile, slack-jawed, like a beast of the field, his mouth hanging open, as I once heard Brother Luke say, but not within Bernard's hearing, the better to catch flies; his soul was for once alive, or at least apparent.

In the centre of it all was their leader, a degraded cleric dressed all in black, with long hair around his bald mockery of a tonsure, croaking out words of blasphemy, lament and scorn. His whole existence was a kind of leer at God's creation: I have seen no eagle, but we found a crow, coughing, as he delivered a profane sermon to chastise a member of his band who had tossed aside a coin,

71

Do not despise the half-penny! With a half-penny you can buy a loaf of bread or plenty of coal and wood to cook your meal and warm your bones, or butter or lard or oil or fat to make your peas taste good, or that hefty serving girl over there, to warm your body and your bed, or a big measure of wine, filled to the top. We drink to Paris! Where a half-penny-worth of wine would cost two pence anywhere else.

And then he took to his feet to dance, his black cloak fluttering around him as he sailed and spun with his cup held high.

His unholy band joined him, and serving maids, and Brother Bernard was dancing among them in a kind of blasphemous ecstasy, and I hope that Brother Andrew's face was not a mirror my own, because on it mixed in with the horror at their shamelessness was a kind of fascination, an enchantment. I stood on a table, I preached and I prayed. I put before them the example of Aurelian who, in his lusts, danced himself to death. The Devil is the inventor and governor and disposer of dances and dancers, leading vain folk who are like thistledown wafted on the blast, or the dust which the wind lifts from the face of the earth, or clouds without water, which are carried about by winds. But the music and the song and the dancing were too strong for my words. I stood on the table, shaking from the vibrations of the dancers' feet, my words ignored.

The tumult subsided, but not because of anything I had done, but because the next part of this unholy service was to occur, and it was by far the worst, the blackest mockery, the words of it, blasphemous and obscene; I would shrink from relating it were it not that I have bound myself to recording all the events of our days; and should anyone happen to read this, let this serve as a warning against the unholy excesses of man and demon, which in this place seemed conjoined.

Their leader, their crow, led what he called a hymn.

> *Thrust, tongue, into the mystery*
> *Of the glorious body*
> *And lick the precious flux*
> *The price that Christ*
> *Our noble fruit of lust*
> *Paid spilling into the world*

And his respondents rejoined,

> *Amen. Alleluia.*

In the horror of it we trusted to Brother Bernard's higher nature to resist this foulest of blasphemies, and he was getting to his feet, I am sure to denounce the crow – and we were going towards our brother, to support him, but before the denouncement could issue from Brother Bernard's mouth, one of the members of the debased company was on his feet, pointing to the three of us, and he said that we were the Pope's Friars, the Pope's Demons, and we carried great treasure we had stolen from a cathedral, and the three of us, as all turned our way, were united again, and we ran.

Saint Francis said,

Many sorrows and many woes will that wretched man have, who sets his desire and his heart and his hope on earthly things, for the which he abandons and loses the things of heaven, and at the last will also lose these things of earth. The eagle flies high: but if she had a weight tied to her wings, she could no more fly high; so man for the weight of earthly things cannot fly high, to wit, cannot attain to perfection; but the wise man, that ties the weight of remembrance of death and of judgement to the wings of his heart, cannot by reason of his great fear go astray and fly among the vanities and the riches of this world, the which are the cause of damnation.

And Brother Bernard said,

That man, who you called the Crow, his followers called the Poet, he had a different gospel. He says that there was a prophet, an unhappy man named Gottschalk, who was persecuted and martyred for this faith, who taught that all is determined. Before we are born, it is fixed whether we go to heaven or hell, so it matters not what we do in this life because our path into the next has already been fixed.

And Brother Andrew said,

Each night I battle against temptation.

Oh my Master. How I wish I was home with you. I should not seek to roam.

. . .

Saint Vitus's Day

Vitus's father often whipped him because his son despised the idols of Rome and refused to worship them. He tried to change his son's mind by offering him music and sporting girls and other kinds of delights. Then he shut the boy up in his bedroom and a wonderful fragrance came out of it. The father looked through the door and saw seven angels around his son and exclaimed, The gods have come to my house! and was immediately struck by blindness.

They took Vitus's father to the temple of Jove and promised a bull with gilded horns for the recovery of his sight, but he remained blind. Then he begged his son to obtain his healing, and at the son's prayer the father saw the light again. When even then he did not believe, but rather thought to kill the child, an angel appealed to Vitus's tutor, Modestus, and commanded him to take the boy in a boat and go to another land. While they were at sea, an eagle brought them their food, and they wrought many wonders when they landed.

Arousing the jealousy of the pagans, Vitus suffered martyrdom when he was only twelve years old.

We are hungry. We have lost track of the days. Like the sinning sheep that has wandered from the flock, we have lost our way.

Saint Mark and Saint Marcellian's Day or Saint Joseph of Arimathea's Day

Saints Mark and Marcellian were twin brothers who were martyred in Rome for their faith. They were nailed upside down to pillars, and their great devotion endured. Saint Joseph of Arimathea buried Our Lord and was immured inside a city wall of Jerusalem as punishment from the Jews but was comforted by divine light and fed with food from heaven.

The woods are thick and deep and the birds mock us from their trees. We are not sure if today is a Friday or a Saturday, but we fast anyway, although we have no choice because we do not have any food.

The Feast of the Holy Martyrs Gervasius and Protasius

Augustine relates in the twentieth book of his *On the City of God* that a young man was bathing his horse in the river when suddenly a demon took him, tormented him, and threw him in the river as if he were dead. In the evening, vespers were sung in the nearby church of the Holy Martyrs, and the young man, as if struck by voices, did run into the church screaming and clung to the altar as if he were tied to it and no power could pull him away. The demon was conjured to go out of the man but threatened to tear him limb from limb if he should be banished from the poor young man's body. When the demon finally was expelled, one of the young man's eyes hung down his face by a thin vein, but they put the eye back in its place as well as they could, and in a few days, by the merits of Gervasius and Protasius, the young man was completely cured.

When we see peasants in villages, they watch us. They always watch us. They look up from their work to make shrewd judgements of our condition. Are we angels or demons? outlaws? thieves, victims, despoilers? Might we be in the service of a powerful lord, whose men would take vengeance upon any injuries that befell us? Or are we carrying our burden as a great gift to anyone who would trouble himself to take it?

Others watch us as the beasts of the field watch the rain, their state too unalterable for anything to be profit or wonder. They wait only for food or the slaughter man.

One man gave us food. He knew that it was a feast day but it did not trouble him that he did not know its name.

I have discovered why there are pages missing from my chronicle. I had stretched out to sleep, but sleep was not permitted me. When my eyes were shut, images of the past days returned unbidden to my vision, the blasphemous Crow, the Crown of Thorns in its perpetual light, Brother Andrew's face when he whispered to me. When my eyes were open they wished only to be shut. The fire we had made for ourselves was close to extinguishing, and I watched the colours and the shapes, hoping in this way to be lulled towards sleep. And my attention was taken by a scratching that I at first took to be the sound of an animal making its timid nest in the hollow of a tree. But when I looked past the fire I saw Brother Bernard beside its dying light, certain that he was unobserved, leaning over one of my fragments with a pen that I thought had been lost, with ink that is precious to me, cutting into the page, obliterating my words.

Saint Silverius's Day

I shall try to write the tidings of the day in the order in which they occurred, so that their history will be a kind of mirror of the events of the day as we experienced them, and any reader, my Father, my Master, my Lord, will be given an accounting of how these things occurred and why we reacted to them the way that we did, and in this way, perhaps our blame shall be lessened; and in this way too I might myself begin to understand why and how these things occurred.

We had walked through the forest, and reached an abbey where once presided the logician Abelard's great enemy. They offered us food and drink, which we accepted, even

Bernard, despite his dislike of Cistercians. And in this place, Brother Bernard told me of his penitence at stealing my parchment and ink, but when I asked him to what ends he was making of them, he did not answer me. We accepted the gifts of monks and made some more ink, to replace what Bernard had stolen, and when we were done, and I was thanking the monks, Brother Bernard had stolen some of that too.

And we had walked on, recovering our path, finding again the Via Francigena. And in our relief at finding again the right road, at anticipating the night we would spend in a pilgrims' hospice, where the sawdust on the floor would be as welcome to us as a potentate's mattress, we sang as we walked, like soldiers, like children, the rhythm of our words matching the rhythm of our steps, so that all was praise.

As the sun began its descent, we reached a village. It was a village much like any other, so I have no means of warning anyone away from it. It had a few ragged fields of barley, a dead crow hanging in each field as a warning to any others of their tribe should they attempt to eat the crops, a pond, a barn, a patch of grass in the middle, within some small low habitations. The villagers were curious as we approached. They invited us to drink and to eat, and we sat in their grass that was in the middle of the village and we accepted their hospitality and tried to deflect the interest that was coming our way.

They took us for penitents, and then they concluded that one of us had committed a great sin and the other two were his guards, and then they fell into dispute and could not agree if we were all criminals, or angels sent to direct them, or demons sent to test them.

And I did not know then and I still do not know if their

suspicion of us as demons was a game they were playing, or if it was truly felt, something caught on the wind that registers deep in the soul, because the superstition and fear of villagers can be a great and terrible potency, but their strongest men took hold of us, and they interrogated us as to our motives and our true nature.

They had a kind of priest among them, a man with a wildness about him, as if he had stared for too long into a consuming fire.

Look at the demons, they could almost be ordinary men, said one of his followers.

Except there is always something wrong about them, the wild priest said. That one is too large, that one too beautiful. In his attempt to mock the angels, he gives himself away.

And that one?

Too pale, too ordinary. Have you ever seen a youth who looks less noticeable?

They proceeded to taunt us. Come on demons! one of them said. Extend your power against us.

We are not demons, I told them.

Prove it.

Oh my Master, you have taught me many things, but not how a man may prove his innocence.

They tied us up and attached the ropes to stakes of wood in the grass.

Free yourself, demons! they said.

We are not demons, I told them. We are men, like you.

Because they were calling us demons, because they could make as if we were a threat to them and to their village and to their low crops, that gave them the excuse to look through our bags and there was nothing we could do to stop them. They found the treasures I had gathered and they threw them around, as if they were worthless, although some thought them proof of our sorcery, and they affected still to believe that we were inspired by the Devil to stop their crops and bring a blight upon them, but they were, as Brother Bernard shouted out to them before they stopped his mouth with foul rags, simple thieves.

I do not know if I understand anything, if the unworthy capacities that impressed my Master are merely a trick of mimicry and memory. Numbers are shapes that I can repeat and multiply; but maybe they signify nothing outside of themselves. Without correspondence in my heart or spirit, their true essence goes untouched. My Master uses his intellect as an instrument to apprehend holy truths and deliver them to those that can use them best; mine is a performance to impress an audience, to plead, not quite to pray. Except, when I was in the witness of my harshest audience yet, harsher than my Master, harsher even than the Principal, I failed.

And covered by darkness, the solitary tolling of a bell, and a new sound rose to our ears, a slow heavy clinking, engine of hell. But this is wrongly told, I am leaping ahead of my story, how may I switch from day to night, it was still daylight, our interrogation proceeded, we were powerless except for the infinite mercy of God.

Cupidity and avarice overcame their superstition and supposition, and they decided after all that we were criminals carrying a great treasure. When we were hungry they did not feed us, when we were thirsty they did not give us water, instead they spat at us some of the beer they were drinking, and then sat together away from us as if they were frightened they had gone too far and maybe we were demons after all, the Pope's Friars, who might enact a terrible revenge.

Then came the sound of him, and he arrived in the

torchlight, our old enemy, the malevolent Simeon the Palmer. After that, even at this remove, I have difficulty in remembering the events in the order that they occurred. Simeon was wary of us, but he knew what he desired. And I understand now that it was in that first moment of our meeting, when he saw my hand go to the scrip in which I carry my Master's Great Work, that he had decided what he would steal from us.

That was not all they took. They took the apparatus to demonstrate to the Pope, and they threw aside the rest of our things, the bundle of rags that my Master had given me for when we had lost all hope, and the treasures that I had gathered and which they did not have the eyes to see, and the writings I have made, because they have no interest in them. And they drove us out of their village and we sat on a hillside by a stream and Brother Bernard, like a beast, knelt on all fours and drank from the stream to try to wash away the foul taste of the rags, and this was the time of the greatest sorrow.

Which we made worse, by chiding one another. We had failed and I was unable to consider any course of action, because I was thinking about our return and my Master's face when I would tell him of our failure, all his great hopes gone.

My companions told me that I should open the package that my Master gave me. This was even though they had lost all respect for my powers and my leadership and, by extension, my Master's authority and wisdom were becoming null. But in time of no hope, fleeting comfort may be found in even the slightest possibility of a change of state. The sky was dark, a sliver of moon above us, the North Star, and I ripped the cloth with Brother Bernard's knife.

I do not know what I was expecting. My fingertips

recognised it instantly, but my understanding tarried behind. I had to hold it, open it, feel the fall of the pages, some few of which have been inscribed by me. I told them,

It is my Master's Book.

Both my companions asked what then was in the box that the Palmer had stolen. I think some of my authority was already returning, but I did not give an answer because it was at that moment that the night was torn apart. A crack of thunder as loud as the trumpets at Jericho sounded, followed by screams of fear, the noises of consternation and confusion, villagers running below as if the Devil himself were riding them.

I returned to the empty village with my reluctant companions and saw there the wreckage of the shining box that the Palmer had stolen and the smell of sulphur from the firecracker that my providential Master had placed beneath its lid.

We gathered what was left of our possessions and returned to the road, walking by starlight, and when my companions asked why they were chosen for this journey, I answered that I had chosen them, because they were the two members of our Order that I loved the best.

And this is what happened on this day, Saint Silverius's Day, the twentieth day of June in the year of Our Lord 1267.

. . .

Saint Bartholomew's Day

Bartholomew the apostle went to India, which is at the end of the earth. He entered a temple wherein there was an idol named Astaroth, in whom dwelled a demon who claimed that he healed the sick. In truth he did not cure them but merely stopped hurting them.

Brother Bernard is suffering. When his bowels emptied again, he cried aloud. He slunk away from the fire and we heard the sound again, like a sudden burst of rain. Throughout the night we had been often woken by the mournful repetition of Bernard stumbling from his sleeping place to the trees and whining as his bowels washed open. In between these dismal occurrences he rolled on the ground and spoke out loud in waking sleep,

Have mercy on me, O Lord, for I am in distress. I am like a dead man.

I said, to comfort him,

Stand firm and you will be saved.

He was not to be comforted. In his anguish, his tongue found a new nimbleness,

Tears and affliction have washed my eyes, my throat, my belly. Demons have broken my strength.

I had the means to assuage his torment but not at first the will. I have saved some of the treasures I have collected but these were intended for the studies of my Master, not the soothing of my companion's pain. But then, for love of Brother Bernard, and pity for his suffering, I instructed Andrew to fetch water from the stream, which we boiled inside a pot on the fire. I tore blackberry root and chamomile leaves and ground them to a paste which I poured into the pot and brought Bernard towards it.

I have seen something great, he said. It was like the window we saw.

Breathe in the vapour, I said to him.

It was like the window but not of glass, it was an enormous wheel the size of a village, divided into chambers, and it was rolling before me on the crest of a hill.

Move your head, I said.

I thrust his face closer to the water but he kept speaking.

It was built of wood, and each of the chambers contained an inhabitant, a prisoner, and the one that I was looking at, that had fixed my attention, that compelled it, was in the top corner, between a man who was laughing and another who was crying.

While the water is still hot, I said.

And the chamber was empty. It was the only one that was empty in the whole structure. The chamber was empty and it was meant for me.

I thrust his face close to the pot of water, instructed him to breathe slowly and deeply. He tried to speak, he coughed, I moved his head closer to the curative vapour.

His breathing subsided, he quietened, he breathed.

In my guilt at not immediately helping my companion, the remedy I made for him was too strong. For, as my Master has written, in whatsoever thing the most High God has put an admirable virtue, He has also placed a hurt, to be as it were the guard of the thing itself.

And maybe the ingredients had not been well judged, and maybe the powder had not been finely enough ground, for, instead of assuaging Brother Bernard's torment, my medicine increased it. The fever took him to a place beyond words to describe it. The poison and its remedy fought against each other on the battleground of his body. We watched over our companion for the rest of the night and most of the following day. I assured Brother Andrew that our friend would not die.

• • •

84

In the rain we walk, newly baptised, the sorrow and tears of the sinner, contemplating Christ's sacrifice and our own unworthiness.

Sedulius wrote,

To go to Rome, much labour, little profit. The King whom you desire, if you do not bring Him with you, you will not find.

Come quickly, Lord, cut into the various secret hidden passions, open the wound quickly lest the noxious humour spread, cleanse all that is fetid with a pilgrim bath.

· · ·

We walk because we always walk. We sleep because we sometime sleep. We pray, because God loves us.

It was one of those occasions when we could not bear to go on, when one of us, weaker or more sincere, spoke for the rest. Andrew sank to the earth, found a hollow beneath a tree. He said,

We can stay here, we can preach to the birds and the wolves, like Francis.

He pulled a low branch over himself, as cover.

Delightful as it might be to sink into the warm earth, we had to go on. And I had to blandish my companions to do so.

Andrew said,

We can fish in the river. It is good here.

We walk in Our Lord's footsteps. If He stumbles and falls under His load, if He seeks comfort from the basest thief, then His lowly followers, and unworthy believers, can hardly do less. Each step of His was agony. He borrowed from us the capacities for pain and death; in return He gave us eternal life.

But, we rested. Brother Andrew was tired. Brother Bernard

has still not regained his former strength. We lay on the soft earth and looked up to the clouds.

That is like a long-shanked man lying on his side, I said.

Rather, it is a dragon, puffing smoke, and see how it changes, become a valley in the hillside.

Brother Bernard's imagination is inflamed from his sickness.

Brother Andrew sees only clouds. Most marvellous, he says.

And now she is a woman on her back, and there is a fire beside her and the smoke is a forest of trees.

We watch and listen in a kind of wonder, as our companion, like a far traveller, reports back from the worlds he witnesses. These are more true to him than the one that holds us, that stains his lips with the sap from the grass he chews on. Or maybe it is not his sickness that operates his fancy; Brother Bernard's eyes are clear, his brow is free from sweat. My medicine has finally worked, despite its penalty and pain. He lies on his back and without labour of thought the shapes in the sky are named, described, reconfigured.

We have to be careful. The legend, of the Pope's Friars or the Pope's Magicians, travels much faster than we do.

. . .

Saint John the Baptist's Day

By the zeal of his preaching and the meritorious example of his life, the holy forerunner of Our Lord converted many. The prudent good judgement that Saint John the Baptist brought to his preaching came out in three ways. First, he used threats to put fear in the perverse, saying, Now the axe is laid to the root of the tree, every tree that does not bear good fruit is cut down and thrown into the fire. Second, he used promises to entice the good, saying, Repent, for the kingdom of heaven is at hand. Third, he used moderation, attracting the sinful towards perfection little by little, imposing light obligations to carry them forward to greater things – the people at large to do works of mercy, the tax collectors to abstain from hungering for what belonged to others, the soldiers not to rob anyone or accuse anyone falsely, and to be satisfied with their wages.

Lighted torches are carried around the bonfire on his feast day, because the Baptist was a burning torch and a shining torch. A wheel is spun because around John's birth the days become shorter, just as at Christ's birthday the days become longer. As Saint John said, I must decrease but He must increase.

The false book was bound in red leather with two ribs on the spine. I had thought that this signified the earth and heaven, the two natures of man, as well as reaching back to our originals, Adam and Eve, while suggesting too the book's author and its intended reader, united together in a common purpose, yet necessarily apart. The false book was destroyed by the cupidity of demons and villagers, and the sulphur and saltpetre of my Master's precautions.

My Master does not reach towards analogical meaning. He observes, he reads, he demonstrates, he proves. His thought is never airy. But now, his Book dispatched, maybe now, alone in the room at the top of the friary, no scribe, no pupil, his friends all too far away, endeavours temporarily over, prayers said, night drawn close, maybe then he permits something of the fancy into his mind; his ferocity relaxes, that stern hold he has on the world, on himself, abates, maybe too he permits himself to receive unbidden images into his mind, phantoms of possibility, Popes and kings bow to him, a grateful world at last acknowledges his eminence in winding lines that stretch out from the word in red and azure. Maybe he even permits himself to feel some concern for his unworthy messenger and his labour.

On the pages, inside the four packages that contain the seven parts of the Book, inscribed no less clearly than the words and numbers and the mathematical figures in the margins, are the sternness and authority of my Master. The copyist, when my Master's attention was away from the work, gave space to his fancy, colouring in red the large initial letter to announce that a new subject is to be discussed, and then switching colours, using the knife to cut in new shapes, the threads of his fancy, winding towards the edges of the page in blue. Lines rounden, loop, droop, curve. I have looked for meaning here in the copyist's shapes. After a while, one line becomes my Master's face seen from the side, another a leaf dripping like water from a narrow branch. It is as when I was back in the friary with my map to the Holy Land, and my eyes lifted away from the journey to the celestial city to make shapes out of shadows.

But I do not have my companion Brother Bernard's capacity for transformations. And the simplest conclusion is usually the correct one. The two spines of the false book were a means of holding the explosive materials beneath the leather cover. And there is no meaning here, it is just shape without content. The author is unrelenting, the copyist complains and produces a series of blue ornamentations fevered by his weariness at producing those regular cramped letters. He was rushed in execution and made mistakes. I have corrected some of them but I doubt that I have caught them all, the Book is so large, so compendious, so many small words on so many pages.

And perhaps Bernard's designs are no different, his strange shapes inscribed on my pages, a compulsion to make something different. In Bernard's secret drawings are the copies he makes of leaves and trees and animals we have seen on our way and even some men. And then something compels him to combine them, to match the body shape of one with the features of another, the trunk of a tree, a head of a boar, hair of leaves. A butterfly's body has a bird's beak and a lizard's tail. Trees have antlers instead of branches. A bush blossoms wolf-heads for flowers. He is ashamed each occasion his drawings are discovered. You shall not make graven images. It is a blasphemy to rewrite God's creation.

. . .

My companions interrogated me about the journey. They had been discussing it between themselves. They might even have been thinking of forsaking it. This journey has been a lie, Brother Bernard said. Why did you not trust us? Brother Andrew said. What is this Book that we are carrying? It must have great value if other people should desire it so much, Brother Bernard said. Not people, demons, Brother Andrew said. The Devil was in the priest as he was in Simeon the Palmer as he was in that master of your festivities in Paris.

Bernard will not have that. His tongue was thick again, he had not the fluency to convey his passion or his heart, but he will not have us abuse the Crow whom he calls the Poet.

And as we argued, as the night fell and settled around us,

as I explained the importance of the mission, and again, as in my meditations in the friary, as with the copyist's errant hand, my thoughts turned to the castle girl with whom Brother Andrew... I may not ask him, although I long to, as he, I know, wishes to be asked, so he may talk about her again, her beauty, their sin.

Caesarius of Heisterbach teaches that,

Demons are called tempters, because they are either the authors or provokers of all the temptations that draw me into sin. If the Devil tempted the first man in Paradise, if he presumed to tempt Christ in the desert, what man is there in the world that he will leave untempted? To every man there are assigned two angels, the good for protection, the evil for trial.

The Lord your God tries you, that it may appear whether you love Him.

$$\bullet \ \bullet \ \bullet$$

Saint Peter's Day
or it might be Saint Paul's Day

We have lost our way again, so we navigate by churches. We stay away from villages because of what happened to Brother Andrew.

The head of the church lies to the east. The north is cold and dark. The south is where the sunshine pours in. We are heading south. We beat our way through branches and thorns, church to church, bell by bell.

Outside farmyards geese chase us.

Brother Bernard has learnt gentleness. It might be the example of Brother Andrew, or even my own, or it might be the effect of his fever, but he no longer exhibits that bellicosity of former times; he reflects Our Lord's gentleness and this is to the profit of his soul but all the same it makes me more timid on our road without the promise of his strength to protect us.

In the maps I used to follow there were castles and rivers and shrines and nothing in between. Life on this part of the journey is the other way around. It is in the nullity that the mapmaker could not imagine that the true things are to be found. And where we are, our small progress, the worms and seeds of food that sustain us, like Church fathers in the wilderness, preaching to the insects and the stars.

As it is written, With labour and toil shall you eat thereof all the days of your life. Thorns and thistles shall bring it forth to you; and you shall eat the herbs of the earth.

Ahead of us are the mountains.

. . .

Saint Swithin's Day

Saint Swithin directed full well the bishopric of Winchester and among the good things he did for his people, paid for out of his own pocket, was the construction of a stone bridge on the west side of the town. One time there came a woman over the bridge with her lap full of eggs, and a certain man, who was reckless and violent, fought with her, and broke all her eggs. And it happened that the holy bishop came that way and he bade the woman let him see her eggs, and he lifted his hand and blessed those eggs, and they were made whole, each one.

Why did the man fight with her? Brother Bernard said.
Maybe he desired her eggs, Brother Andrew said.

Maybe he desired her, Brother Bernard said.

I admonished them that in their speculations about the particulars of the story, they had moved away from its moral, of which, if we were to preach it, we would intend our listeners to apprehend the greatness of the bishop Saint Swithin, his capacity for miracles, but above all to remark how he, like Christ with sinners, had the power to heal something that was broken, to make it whole.

I would like some eggs, Brother Bernard said.

• • •

We have found our way again, returned to the pilgrim route. We are not always welcome. The truth we represent does not reflect well on the comfortable prelates of the towns. Some gates are closed to us and we sleep outside, in the shelter of the city wall.

When we preach, Andrew begins, I proceed, and Bernard makes response, and in such a way we gather and hold a congregation.

> *The Lord be with you.*
> *And with your spirit.*
> *Lift up your hearts.*
> *We will lift them up to the Lord.*
> *Let us give thanks to the Lord.*
> *It is right and just.*

A deformed beggar called us mad. Or he may have been calling himself mad. It was difficult to understand the tongue he spoke. I was looking anyway at the watchtowers the lords of the region have built on to the ramparts of the town. I could not decide if this was to guard the town from its enemies or to watch over their own people.

In the morning we were permitted entry through the gate. We begged for alms and received food, which we ate on the city ramparts looking over the valley towards the mountains, whose tops, like rough broken knifes, cut into the clouds, which bleed and stain the mountains white; and the heart sinks with dread and the mind lifts with wonder to gaze upon places so high, where, it is a superstition to think this I know, God seems to be closer.

• • •

We took a path away from the road to follow a track of sage. My companions did not understand my excitement, but I was able to persuade them to follow, although I had to keep persuading them. Maybe it was because of the enthusiasm with which I delivered my argument, but it was as if the universe had to be perpetually made and remade, and my companions would only heed my direction if I gave the argument perpetually. When I relented, they dawdled; when I argued again, we walked faster. I told them that this is a treasure, never found in our country, seldom in this one. I told them that this had been found and planted and it had flourished under wise oversight. The sage grew thicker the further we had gone away from our road, which we could no longer see behind thorn trees and bushes of monk's pepper.

And now we have arrived at this garden, and nothing could be more pleasing, judiciously moderated plenty, there is wisdom here and peace, the earth and the heavens mapped out, in miniature.

The gardener is Father Gabriel, who is a man of modest manner, white-haired, beardless. He possesses the power my Master calls fascination. A superior soul impresses another, a superior intelligence impresses its inferiors, some say that through such an impression one could throw a camel into a pit by sight alone.

His herb garden is plotted in rectangles which are full of treasures. Sage, rue, southernwood, poppy, pennyroyal, mint, parsley, radishes, and, for love's sake, on the other side of the wall, gladioli and lilies and roses. The fruit trees are in bloom.

At the centre is a perfect square with a round pool and a pentagonal fountain, demonstrating mathematical order and divine grace, earth and spirit, an Eden.

I do not know if I could find this place again. We stumbled upon it, at the end of a day, following a track of sage.

Where is the promised treasure? Brother Bernard said.

I have it in my bags.

He has enchanted you.

My companions are impatient to leave. It is as if they are my Master's chosen messengers and I am the additional one, their cause of vexation, who needs to be told of his obligation.

· · ·

The villagers are timid of Father Gabriel's power. They do not like to come to his garden to see its foundations. On our second day a young woman did come to consult him, escorted by an even younger man, who walked several paces behind her and never spoke a word. But, every few days Father Gabriel makes a tour of outlying villages to visit the sick and the declining.

He invites me to accompany him. The invitation does not extend to my companions, who occupy themselves in a show of making preparations to leave.

Father Gabriel and I walk together, away from the garden, which he takes one look back at before our path departs from it, as if he were confirming the mark of it in his memory in case God should decree that he never sees it again.

We are taken into an old man's house, which is divided into small sleeping quarters. The stable, which is part of the house, beside the kitchen, underneath the loft, contains straw for the donkey and a blanket for the old man. He used to sleep in the main house, before his eldest son got married. His wife still sleeps in the main house, in the same bed as one of her unmarried daughters. It was this daughter who took us in there to tend to her mother, white hair loose, face ennobled by her disease. Purified through pain, she was like a paper lantern; her soul, about to be untethered, shone through the skin.

Father Gabriel made a medicine for her, of iris flowers and caraway seeds broken in wine and after taking it she shivered, and he asked me to hold her, and I held her. I have never held a woman before. She was so narrow and light as if her substance was made of air. My touch made her shiver and she kept on shivering and I made to let her go but Father Gabriel instructed me to keep holding her and he said that was half of the medicine.

• • •

The full moon rises over Father Gabriel's garden. We sit on the highest elevation, a chair of raised turf, where we look over the whole garden and then, therefore, the universe. The mind moves on wings as the Lady Philosophy of Boethius promised, mounting the air and soaring beyond the clouds, rising to the eighth sphere of stars. And maybe beyond, the Primum Mobile, and all of this is God, my home, my source, my ending.

The master gardener has no urgency about him. There is

a comfort in his presence as if he is in harmony with his own trees. And how I should like to stay here, to tend the land, to make things grow, to listen to the complaints of the village people, to heal them.

In the distance, I see my companions walking again along the track of sage towards our former road. They are bent under the weight of the bags they carry, which used to be divided amongst three.

Stay here, the wise man says.

And who knows what he has known and what he has been before he became holy. A shovel is heavy; a sword is heavier. I do not believe that it is entirely his labours on the land that have made him so strong.

You are good at this. I have prayed for the Lord to send labourers into His harvest.

He looks over the walls of the garden, towards mountains and clouds. My companions stumble and go on.

The harvest is great, but the labourers are few. And I shall need a successor.

I tell him that I am sworn to my Master's will.

Let your companions fulfil your mission. I will teach you all I know. One man in a thousand might be capable of receiving my instruction.

I would not be here were it not for my Master.

And yet, I find it hard not to compare these men, and the match is made not entirely to Father Gabriel's prejudice. He has patience, good humour and strength; his heart beats in rhythm to the seasons. And my Master, he always stands outside, with his anger and envy and pride.

I am invited to remain here, to learn the skills of husbandry, to meditate here and to work here, and nothing could be more accordant. There is wisdom here, and peace. You are the seal of the image of God, full of wisdom and perfect in beauty. You have been in Eden, the garden of God; every precious stone was your covering: the sardius, the topaz, and the jasper, the chrysolite, and the onyx, and the beryl, the sapphire, and the carbuncle, and the emerald: gold the work of your beauty.

I feel unburdened. I can trust my companions to satisfy the commission, or at least attempt it, without stint.

Father Gabriel quotes the word of Saint Anthony,

Sit in your cell and your cell shall teach you all things.

I must fulfil my mission.

And wise Abbot Luan, Dig and sow that you may have wherewith to eat and drink and be clothed, for where there is sufficiency, there is stability, and where there is stability there is religion... Hunger is too hard a stepmother to learning.

In this little Eden, these loved squares of earth are a pathway to the celestial kingdom. The flowers, the herbs, even the monksbane. My Master would approve the rhubarb and rue.

I may not. I am bound to complete my mission.

He asks me to tell him the nature of my mission, and I am put into confusion. His fascination demands the entirety of truth and yet something inside of me wishes to withhold, as if once released of it, I shall be emptied.

My Master has written a Book. I am bound to deliver this Book to its intended audience, its reader.

Who is?

I may not say.

What are the contents of the Book?

Truth. Wisdom. The meanings of past and future times, the details of the construction of devices that some men might call miraculous. These are just some of the contents of the Book.

He looks at me. I may not look at him. He could overpower me if he chose, with his body or his will.

He quotes another,

It is in the cloister that Bernard of Clairvaux says, the monk comes to find the Heavenly Jerusalem, the true destination of any and all pilgrimages.

I have read him. My Master has shown me his writing.

What then is the city?

It is like being back in the friary, performing for the Principal and visiting dignitaries. Except here the only audience is Father Gabriel, the owls nesting, his garden.

The city is itself only an image, a figure of the future Heavenly City: and the journey to it is made not by proceeding with feet but with feelings –

And if you could? Would you stay?

I would be tempted.

I am not tempting you. I am offering you something. Nature surpasses art without strife or anxiety. But maybe I still suffer from vanity and it stretches this far: I do not wish my flowers to die or my walls to come down. Without care, any place can become like any other.

My name is John the Pupil. I do not have the right to change teachers. No man can serve two masters. Maybe I can return, after my mission is complete.

You have made your choice. We will not see each other again, Father Gabriel says.

I will have to travel fast to catch up to my companions.

As it is written, And the Lord God sent him out of the paradise of delights, to till the earth from which he was taken.

And if I have been enchanted, as my companions said, then nothing is as I see it.

Through the senses, as through windows, vices creep into the soul. Therefore, remove yourself from the temptations of the city and of nature; gaze not upon those agencies of sin that might ensnare you; even to meditate upon the pleasant rivers and streams, where the birds chirp and living pools mirror the sky, and the brook babbles on its way, and many other things entice men's ears or eyes; lest through the luxury and abundance of plenty a soul's strength be turned to weakness, and its modesty be violated. For indeed it is unprofitable to gaze frequently on that whereby you may one day be caught, and to accustom yourself to such things as you shall afterwards scarce be able to lack. Plato himself, though he was a rich man, whose costly couch Diogenes once trod under his muddy feet, chose the Academe, a villa far from the city, and not only solitary but pestilent also, as the proper place for the study of philosophy; that the assaults of lust might be broken by the anxiety and frequent presence of sickness, and that his disciples might feel no other delights save in those things that he taught them.

• • •

Saint Thomas of Canterbury's Day

The martyr, at whose shrine we have worshipped, suffered for the Church, in a church, a holy place, at sacred prayer, among his priests, in order to illustrate both the holiness of the one who suffered and the cruelty of his persecutors.

There are many miracles attested to Saint Thomas. By his merits, the blind did see, the lame did walk, the deaf did hear, the dead were brought back to life. A bird that had learned to speak was being chased by a hawk, and cried out the phrase it had been taught, Saint Thomas, help me! The hawk fell dead and the bird flew on.

As for the saint's killers, the wrath of God dealt with them. One gnawed his fingers to bits; others became slavering idiots; some were stricken with paralysis; others went mad and perished miserably.

After days in the garden, our feet have healed and we have grown softer again. The way is hard, uphill, rest only in a shepherd's shelter. We walked towards the mountains and it was as if they refused us. They grew no larger, although it appeared to me that we were getting smaller.

We all have sticks now. I think that Bernard has his eye on mine, but I know that if I offer to exchange them, he will think himself to have the worst of the bargain.

This morning, when finally the mountains had consented to allow us to reach them, we had spread out. It was unspoken, but it was one of those cases, that occur increasingly often, I think, when we are content to walk alone with the company only of our own thoughts, while knowing that our companions are not far from hand. I came upon Bernard. He was standing still, looking up at the mountains and pulling at his nose. It took me a little while to understand that he was weeping. I had not thought him capable of such holiness.

Brother Andrew's injuries slow him down, and therefore us. We had intended to cross the mountain into Italy all in one day of climbing but the condition of Brother Andrew does not permit this. Or maybe it would have, if we had found the way to the pass. But we did not, we climbed to what had looked to us like the pass, but we ended beneath a steep cliff and we had to climb down again.

It is cold on the mountainside even with the brightness

of the sun that shines on the stones of this shelter that a thoughtful shepherd has made. There are worlds in each stone, the lines in the rock look like rivers, the lighter patches of brown are fields and woods, the darker are mountains, the darkest are towns, and we are at a dark curve of brown at the top of the world. I could look at it for hours but the light is fading, there is snow under my feet, and I am shivering from the cold and cutting these marks on scraps of parchment without being able to see the words I am making. Brother Bernard keeps stealing from me, but, in guilt or self-reproach, he returns the pages he has defaced, and now that I am running out of writing materials again, I use pages again from before, and I write these words over the shapes of monsters that Brother Bernard has drawn.

Earlier, looking at the mountains, he said to us, It makes you believe that there was a race of giants who lived here.

I did not answer him because Brother Andrew had gathered a handful of snow which he pressed together and then threw at me. I did the same, hurling a handful of snow back at Brother Andrew, as did Brother Bernard. The three of us battled in the snow in this manner until we could no longer find any snow to gather.

And then come and accuse me, said the Lord. If your sins be as scarlet, they shall be made as white as snow. And if I be washed with snow waters, my hands shall shine so clean.

Saint Kilian's Day

Our holy precursor Saint Kilian travelled to Rome with his companions. And from there he went on to Germany, where his preaching converted a great lord. But after he warned the lord that his union to his wife, who was his own brother's widow, was unlawful, the vengeful wife took advantage of her lord's absence to dispatch her soldiers to the town square where Kilian was singing the praises of the Lord with two companions. Kilian exhorted his brothers not to resist the martyr's crown, and they were all three immediately beheaded. When the lord returned, he asked the whereabouts of the servants of God. His wife feigned not to know. But the matter was soon discovered, for the assassin, running about in all directions, complained that Kilian was burning him with a dreadful fire. The assassin tore himself apart with his own teeth. His mistress too soon expired.

My companions and I discussed martyrdom. We all said that we would welcome it but in my unworthy heart I did not believe any of what was said, least of all by me. Brother Andrew, despite the condition of his leg and skin, is too tied to life and the world to cast away either of them. And Brother Bernard, while still a mystery to me, he will always be a mystery to me, alike to a figure carved out of the mountain we climb or one of those trees whose monstrous cousins his imagination compels him to draw, is a part of the world even if his place in it is as much a mystery to him as it is to us. And I am just beginning to gain a fuller love for Creation, because something happened to my senses in Father Gabriel's garden, they were exalted, enlarged (Brother Bernard would say enchanted): I am now able to see the world in its details, to look through Brother Andrew's eyes, to apprehend the will of God as it traced creatures in the mountain forest, drove clouds across the sky, touched my skin.

We were praying outside our shelter, and this should not

be the case but it is, it is easier to give thanks to God on the mountain than in the valley. Brother Andrew threw off his cloak and jumped into a pool of water abutted by rocks and he urged me and Brother Bernard to do likewise. To demonstrate my love for Brother Andrew, I lowered myself into the cold water. Brother Andrew splashed at me and together we splashed at Brother Bernard until Brother Bernard, alone on the rocks, wetter on land than he would have been in the water, finally consented, complaining, to join us.

We were trying to see our future path up through the mountain, and the water that washed us fell down and broke over black rocks that hung over our pool, and the way up looked so evident, but then it had done so yesterday when the mountain confounded us and we had to turn back on our path. We were hungry and cold and lost, but we were joyous, led by Brother Andrew who always loves to be immersed in water. And this is when we became aware of two figures watching us.

The sun was behind them and the shadows they cast over the water made us even colder. We were naked, immodest, like beasts or children. We were also defenceless against the malice of enemies. They wore blue tunics with hoods to cover their faces, and they carried heavy sticks and their shadows were lengthening over us as they reached the side of the pool.

The larger of our pursuers spoke to us first. He asked if any of us had been in a village whose name I did not recognise. When he did not receive assent to this, he asked if we knew a healer by the name of Father Gabriel, and as we were still silent, he spoke more impatiently when he asked if we had stayed in Father Gabriel's garden; and this sounded to us like an interrogation from an assassin who had sufficient scruple to determine that the mark for his malice was the same as the one his masters or confederates had ordered him to kill.

Brother Bernard splashed through the water to get to the side opposite to our interlocutors of whom the slighter shook, as if in tears, as he stumbled with wet hands and feet and knees to climb over the wet stones, falling back submerged into the water, but then it became apparent that it was laughter.

They were not assassins or assailants, and they were not intent on causing us harm. And neither were both men. The one who had been interrogating us was a visiting shoemaker and also a most practised guide through the mountains. He is the grandson of the old woman that we had attended, whom I had held shivering. The other with him is his sister. In their gratitude, taking us as friends of their grandmother's village, they had been directed by Father Gabriel to follow us up the mountain to guard us from any trouble that might befall us.

I write in this way to mimic the knowledge we acquired of our situation as we acquired it, and in this way, in the event of these pages finding their way back to their rightful reader, my Master, the blame that should be apportioned me should I fail might be lessened or at least lightened in understanding and, therefore, maybe, in forgiveness.

• • •

Our guides wear blue tunics as badges of their office. They are careful of us, they slow down their pace for ours, take care to warn us of difficult steps. The sister is hardly less agile and swift than her brother. They climb ahead, but not so far that we will lose sight of one of them, while the other goes on looking for danger before us, falls of rocks and snow.

In the distance between us, we can hardly distinguish one figure in a blue tunic from the other but my heart always lifts when we get nearer and see it is the sister who walks just ahead.

Touching the mountains, walking through the pass, I fell into step with the blue-tunicked mountain girl. Her brother had climbed on, Brothers Bernard and Andrew walked behind. Her hair, cut roughly, could have been a boy's. Her hair is dark and straight, her features sincere and pure, and she has a hint of holiness about her, that sits unevenly with her pride.

That, she said pointing to the highest mountain where dark clouds hid the peak, is where King Romulous lived. He was a miser, who buried an enormous treasure, but no one has ever been able to climb to the top of the mountain, to reach the hoard. The boldest boys of the villages keep trying, they have gone past the stream that cuts through the mountain, they have travelled to the pool of water where the chamois and sheep and goats gather to drink, they have been into the forests, they have reached the meadow that has no name. But the clouds always gather to hide the summit and the boys always have to return, ashamed, older, heavy with care, and each time there are a few who have been left behind, to expire in the clouds.

And then she asked me if I would go with her to find King Romulous's treasure, and if we did, and if we should prosper, what would I do? But before I could answer, she told me what she would do, she would use the riches to restore the prosperity of the village where she lived, whose relic had been stolen, whose lands had spoiled – and then her mood lifted again, she was no longer quite so solemn, and she asked me more questions, about myself and our mission, and I yearned to tell her all things, about my Master, and the Book, and the Pope, and some of the wonders we have seen already, my fears and hopes for the rest of our journey, my father and his goats, my mother who died giving birth to me, the demons who have tried to prey upon us and how we confounded them with the engine of my Master's wisdom and our own sincerity of heart, and the angels who have guarded us, all of whom now in my blasphemous mind wear a blue tunic and have hair cut roughly and short, who have found us and rescued us and taken us back on the right path.

But my tongue was as heavy as ever Brother Bernard's was. I told her my name and I did ask her hers, and she told me that she was called Aude, and she laughed at my name, which sounded to her so heavy and dull, like an old man's grunt. She taught me some words from her native language, which was like French but the words had a rounder, fuller sound, and I asked her about the village where she lived and what had caused the land to despoil, and who had stolen the relic from the church, but all she said was that she was going to attempt a great work and she warned me that I was not to visit her there.

She has made two suppositions about me, which should be contradictory, but which somehow support each other in her mind: one is that I am extremely holy, the other is that I have committed a great sin. Both suppositions rest on the seeming fact of the pilgrimage I am making.

I am unworthy of such respect. I tell her this, but she takes my denial as an indication both of my modesty and my crimes that are so great that only a pilgrimage to Rome may expiate them, and of which nothing else can be said.

I think maybe you would prefer my sister, she says.

Her moods change with the breeze. She is solemn and shy and sometime then giddy and wild. I told her about the spiritual exercises I perform. We must concentrate, walk in Christ's footsteps. Shut your eyes. He will steer you. But Aude gets distracted too easily, birdsong, the sound of water in the stream, the touch of the wind on her face, movements of thought, of feeling, within and without.

I shall never be married, she says. A lady who sleeps with a true lover is purified of all sins. The joy of love makes the act innocent, if it proceeds from a pure heart. Do you have a pure heart? And then she says my name again, making it sound even heavier and duller like a grunt.

But then she sees her brother waiting for us below, and she loses her joy and I say to her,

You could call me Johannes, if you prefer that, or Jean, like the French.

She is not listening. Something reaches her on the air, her eyes widen and she takes my hand.

We shall run down the rest of the way. Just remember not to stop running. If you stop running you will probably fall and die.

Oh my Master, to tell you how I stumbled and fell and flew. It feels so good to be battered and tumbling, to slide down the mountainside startling chamois and sheep and my old friends the goats, who scatter and flee at the fury of our descent. I am light, a cloud rising, a mountain stone falling gathering strength from its descent. Is this how the first men felt? The only difficult step was the first one, to walk towards her, to reach for her, to hurl into space. Once doing it, tumbling down, all will is suspended in the bruising delight of the fall.

Rivers and streams and rocks the shapes of patriarchs and dry river beds and harsh summer gorse and pale lonely flowers on lips of rock and waterfalls and all of it the mountains and my mountain girl. And we ran, tumbling, joyful, not knowing if the sounds we heard are the waters or the thunder on King Romulous's summit, where the boys climb to die, or the sounds that our own bodies make in motion and glee, and the clouds around us like the fog of spirits, stones falling, something miraculous about our progress, occasions when I am running faster than I can believe is possible, and others when it is as if the two of us are entirely still, motionless, the only still point in the universe, and the world and the heavens are hurtling past us and spinning around us, and she told me not to have fear and never to slow, as we fall and roll and get up again, and tumbling and running always, always running.

We came to rest at a waterfall where, after our labours, our glee, we enjoyed a moment of pure peace sun-lit. I think I slept, and it was the arrival of my companions that woke me. I lay stretched out on a rock, head empty, arms and legs out wide. Brother Andrew, who may not resist sensation, jumped from a rock splashing into the water.

Come in! he called. It is very cold!

After some delay, I lowered myself into the water.

Bernard, of course, did not join us. From his place on a rock, he consented to dip his feet into the lower stream, then quickly withdrew them.

Where is the girl? Bernard said.

It was the end of our glee. I climbed out of the water. We looked at the mountain behind, at the valley below, for signs of the blue tunic of her or her brother. I made us walk in three different directions and then another three. We did not find them, only a few blue flowers shivering in the breeze. Our guides had gone, our angels had completed their work and brought us over the mountains and left us on our own again, and I had not thought that heavenly creatures would

have had such capacity for physical joy and so little knowledge of Latin.

Later, Andrew was shivering cold, as if in a fever that was
impossible to dispatch. I warmed him with my body. The
clouds are ghostly low, like fingers of fog, or angels or spirits
lost in the heights trying to grasp hold on to our flesh, before
they slowly break apart and scatter, or we are suffering, the
world is punishing us for consorting with angels and for
having been higher up and faster than man should be.

Saint Anatolia's Day

Anatolia and Victoria were devout sisters whose marriages
had been made to pagan Roman lords. Because the sisters
resisted marriage to non-believers, the suitors denounced
them to the emperor as Christians and received permission
to imprison the sisters on their estates until they had been
convinced to renounce their faith. But the spirit of devotion
was pure and only grew stronger under pains and suffering.
Later, in deadly mockery, a poisonous snake was put in
Anatolia's cell. The snake recognised her goodness and
refused to bite her and so a soldier named Audax was sent
in to kill her instead. The snake set upon the soldier, but
gentle Anatolia intervened to protect him. Such was the effect
of this that Audax converted immediately to Christianity,
and had the joy of being martyred alongside the woman
who had shown him the path to salvation.

My Master wrote,
    He who is ignorant of the places of the world lacks a
knowledge not only of his destination but of the course to
pursue.

We are slowly learning some of the places of the world.

My Master has wondered if the differing peoples of the world vary according to their land. I will be able to tell him about the short men of the hill tribes, the way their bodies are bent to the shape of their climbing, and the longer, narrower men of the plains who stand so much taller. I do not know how much I will tell him about Father Gabriel in his garden, or the angels in the mountains.

My Master will be full of questions for me when we return. I can hear his voice now, slow and insistent:

What is the difference between one people and another? Is there a difference, a change in their build and capacities? What causes it? And when and how do you perceive it? What makes the Savoyards different from the Piedmontese? After all, they share the same mountains. They do not look so different, do they? They eat the same food. How then do you distinguish them and understand the causes of your distinctions?

Do people who eat mutton differ from people who eat beef? Is there a difference in their complexions? Their step? Their capacity of intellect?

Did you notice – no: he will not say that – *What* did you notice about the differences in education in different regions? Did some teachers demand more from their pupils at an earlier age? Were some more severe than others? What effects did the different regimens produce?

And he will ask me about the herbs that I have gathered and the different quantity of sunlight and quality of ground that has enabled each of them to flourish, and he will ask me about the quality of the air, its moistness and dryness, its thickness, gross or troubled, and what these qualities have effected upon the operations of the soul (for a troubled air dejects the soul, saddens it, and blends the humours), and he will ask me about the diversity of beasts, and the manner of terrain that supports them, and he will ask me about the shapes of the leaves of the trees, and the different languages that men speak and whether their understanding of the holy scriptures is different in different regions.

Are the people who live in the mountains happier or freer than those who live in the valleys? Is the shepherd happier than the farmer? It seems so, I will say to my Master, but I do not think it is so much a matter of proximity to farmland or sky or the dryness of their air, more that the shepherd can roam where he may.

And he will ask me about the changes in myself, as if I am an object for my own investigation. He will remark that when I left I was beardless. He will ask if there have been other changes, within and without. He will ask me these questions without mercy but with, I hope, some kindness, as if he too is somehow affected by my changes.

• • •

Saint Veronica's Day

And when Pilate had delivered our Saviour to the Jews to be crucified, it so happened that Tiberius the Emperor fell into a grievous malady. It was told to him that there was one in Jerusalem who cured all manners of illness, so he sent his trusted seneschal to Jerusalem to find this holy healer, not knowing that he was already slain. But the seneschal found Veronica, an old woman and devout, who had been familiar with Jesus Christ. He demanded of her where he might discover the one whom he sought and she wept and said that the one he sought for Pilate had condemned to death. But she said also that when her Lord had still been living, and she had ever occasion to be separated from him, she did paint his image, to always have her with him, to be in his presence, because the figure of his image, despite the proscription against such a thing, did give her much comfort. And when she had told her Lord of this, he requested her kerchief and he held it to his face and he imprinted his divine image as a figure upon it. And the seneschal asked, Is there neither gold nor silver that this figure may be bought with? And Saint Veronica replied, No, but strong of courage, devout and of great affection, I shall go with you and shall bear it to the Emperor for him to see it, and afterwards I shall bring it home again.

The sun shines, we take a voluptuous break. Sitting on the hillside I hear the sounds of birds singing, birds pecking at trees, the wind on the hillside, a boar in the thicket. A horseman rides by. He could be even closer and he still would not see me for I have become part of the land.

To be a hermit is not to renounce, it is to embrace this voluptuous delight and choose not to corrupt it with anything else.

There is a monastery on the very top of one of the mountains behind us. Andrew is stupefied by it, its magnitude, the boldness of the undertaking to have constructed such a thing on high, its grandeur. Brother Bernard is scornful. And the conversation we have about it is made entirely without words.

It was a kind of conquest to get over the mountains but, after the exhilaration and the glee and the tumbling, we still have a long way to go. But we are proved by the road and the weather. We walk with a kind of certainty, usually remembering our modesty when we come to a town. We settle into a rhythm, we can walk for days hardly talking between prayers. And, today, unremarked, we did not perform all the Divine Office. I look at my companions and I know that something has been transacted between us. A bond has been made that will be impossible to break. We are tied to each other, this is something beyond words or gesture. One speaks, but he does not need to finish his sentence, because his companions know what he is going to say, and he knows how each of them is going to respond, and they know how he will respond to their responses, so maybe a few words from the known exchange are uttered, or none at all. Bernard does not condemn the monastery on the mountain as a monument to Cistercian pride, but we hear him anyway, and there is no presumptuousness to this, just a tenderness.

And this would all be good, difficulties and trials behind us, the sun shining upon our journey, of which we have covered more than half the distance, the Book still with us, the model still with us, the fraternity of souls we have planted between us, were it not for the shame I feel, which is beyond scourging or repentance. I am no better than the men of Sodom, to have lusted after an angel.

. . .

Saint Alexis's Day

Alexis was the son of two Romans who were noble yet extremely devout. Three thousand slaves wearing golden girdles and silk clothing waited upon them. Yet, every day Euphemianus set up three tables in his house for the poor and for orphans, for widows and strangers in need. He and his wife Aglaë themselves served at these tables, and did not eat until the last pauper had been fed. Long into their union, their prayers were finally answered and their marriage was blessed with the divine gift of a son, after which the noble couple swore a vow of chastity.

The son was as pious and devout as his parents and when he was seventeen, on his wedding day, he initiated his bride in the miracle of Our Lord, and gave her a golden ring and instructed her to remain a virgin. Then he left Rome and journeyed to the Syrian city of Edessa where he gave away all that he had brought with him and lived the life of a holy mendicant. His bereft father dispatched slaves to every corner of the world to find his son and every day they prayed for him to return.

The holy virgin spoke of the saintly Alexis to the church watchman in Edessa, appearing to him in a vision and saying, Bring me the man of God, because he is worthy of the kingdom of heaven. The spirit of God rests upon him, and his prayer rises like incense in the sight of the Lord. The watchman went to find Alexis, but to escape human glory, Alexis had left the city. He took passage on a boat to Tarsus, but by God's dispensation, a wind blew the boat off course into the port of Rome and, as a foreign pilgrim, he sought alms in his own father's house.

His father gave orders that the stranger be welcomed, and designated a cell for him in the house. Alexis persevered in prayer and disciplined his body with fasting and vigils. The house servants made fun of him and spilled dirty water on his head, but he bore all their insults with unshaken patience. For seventeen years Alexis lived unrecognised in his father's house. Then, knowing by the spirit that the end of his days was near, he wrote out a full account of his life.

On a Sunday, after mass, a voice rang out in the church,

saying, Come to me all you who labour and are burdened, and I will refresh you. All those present had great fear and fell to their knees while the voice sounded again, saying, Seek out the man of God, that he may pray for Rome! They looked around but found no one, and a third time the voice sounded, saying, Look in the house of Euphemianus.

The emperors Arcadius and Honorius, in company with Pope Innocent, came to the house. They found Alexis dead, his face shining like the face of an angel. His father tried to take the writing out of the dead man's hand but could not. The Pope then went up and took the script, which was readily relinquished, and read it before a great throng of people. Euphemianus tore at his garments and pulled at his grey hair and beard, lamenting, Woe is me, my son! Alas, what consolation will I ever find?

And his weeping mother, Aglaë, threw herself upon the body of her only son, and said, My soul's consolation, the one who suckled at my breast, why have you served us so cruelly? Now my mirror is broken and my hope gone. Now begins the grieving that has no end.

And the people standing around heard all this and wept loud and long. For Alexis had been pure in heart and holy in spirit, and his mother and father felt themselves unworthy of him, and yet they reproached their saintly son, because they loved him, and longed for him.

Now the Pope and the emperors placed the body on a princely litter and went before it into the heart of the city. The people all ran to be near the man of God. Any among them who were sick and touched the holy body were cured instantly, the blind received their sight, the possessed were delivered of their demons.

•

We have a new enemy. They are called Ghibellines and they are enemies of the Pope and wish harm to all his friends. Their soldiers roam the countryside in murderous companies, their cities are perilous for any true believers. If they carry banners these show a red cross on a white background. The battlements of their cities are carved like swallows' tails.

Saint Margaret the Virgin's Day

This virgin Margaret had two names, she was called Margaret and Pelagien. Inasmuch as she was named Margaret, she is likened to a flower, for the flower of virginity blossomed from within her. And in that she was called Pelagien, she might be said of *pena*, which means pain, and *lego* or *legis*, to gather. For she gathered pain in a great and cruel manner.

We hear of a holy virgin in an adjacent province, of whom great wonders are told. We would like her blessing. But our way is treacherous, Ghibelline soldiers, Ghibelline towns, that mock the piety of the Pope and all who swear allegiance to him. These are the last times, war within and without. The Tartars drive west, through the gate that Alexander built to shut in the twenty-two kingdoms of Gog and Magog, who Ezekiel prophesied are destined to come forth in the days of the Antichrist. In the Holy Land the Saracens battle against the Lord. The Germans have control of the Pope's kingdom in Italy and seek out his followers to punish.

We remember a time when we had to fight the attentions of robbers who would steal our treasures for brute reward. That seems a more innocent time now. It is a marvel, worthy of my Master's investigation, how lies and rumour and gossip can travel faster than any man. Along with the tales we hear of the holy virgin, in hospices, taverns, monasteries, on hillsides, as we feign to be other than what we are, we hear tales of the magicians of the Pope, clad as friars, who carry a Book that contains the source of all power. The stories differ. Sometime they are a whole army, sometime there are three of them, sometime just one, who looks like a man, who has the devilish power to split himself into multitudes.

Were it not for this uncertainty of the tally, we would be even more in peril than we are. Nonetheless, in the interests of our mission, with the hidden potency of sincerity, we have to be hypocrites and blasphemers. We grant indulgences to men who would murder us if they knew who we are. We pray for their souls and for ours.

And then we find a Guelph town, where we may become ourselves again. There seems no order to this, no boundaries that we may recognise. Some towns are Guelph, most are Ghibelline, and until we see the shape of their battlements and the colour of their flags we do not know if we are entering into the territory of God or His Adversary.

I am diligent. I collect treasures along the way. And sometime, I pick flowers, because I hope to believe that their colours, like emeralds and rubies and amethysts, may have equivalent power to the herbs.

. . .

Saint Victor's Day

It is a hillside village like any other, a few small houses cluster around a church. In front of the church is a plot of grass where the villagers used to graze their pigs. Around the village are vineyards and olive groves. The vines have died and the olive trees grown swollen. The church is empty, and there are fewer villagers than pilgrims, who are thronging to visit the living shrine at the edge of the village.

Outside is a congregation, and an altar. Inside the house is a girl who is saintly. The Devil torments her, Christ consoles her with his stigmata. For a year she has eaten nothing but ginger. The Devil in Advent had hung her naked from a tree.

There are people from the plains here, and the mountains, fine ladies, low serfs, Guelphs and Ghibellines, enmity forgotten in proximity to the holiness of the living saint.

They talk of her, her miracles, her ordeal and her agony and her passion, the news she has brought them from family members that live in distant places, even from across the mountains, although she never leaves her seclusion, and few outside her family are permitted an audience with her. One man tries to sell us cloth that he says has been dipped in the saint's blood, another offers bread that she has chewed and spat out and blessed. A guide in a blue tunic says he can take me to the tree the Devil hung her from. He shakes the leather pouch he wears at his throat.

I have heard these kinds of stories before, the more remote is the district, the greater the claims made for the holiness and sanctity of its saints. Rumours walk faster than men, and grow in remote places. We have been frightened by the legend of the Blind Monk of the Ghibellines, when we should have known better, because we are the subject of another.

Villagers tug at our arms to show the fragments and relics that they are offering to sell. There is one I recognise. Our mountain guide, Aude's brother, in his blue tunic, is taking pennies from pilgrims in exchange for soiled fragments of the saint's clothes. He shows me no recognition, but others in blue tunics block our way so that we are further from the saint's door.

We are not permitted entry into the house. Everything has a price in this village, food and lodging as well as relics of the living saint or the granting of an audience at her shrine. There is no hospice, they have no love for mendicant friars here. When I try to preach to them, of Saint Peter in Chains, and the angel who freed him, they hardly attend my words.

Night grows cold here. I tell my companions that there is nothing for us, that we should drive on with our journey, navigate by the stars, but my companions, Brother Andrew especially, wish to stay here longer, to meet the saint. We need, he says, her blessing on our journey. We pray for guidance on an empty still street, with just a dog for company who waits for scraps at the tavern door.

Perhaps, Brother Bernard says, we should go in there.

Or we should proceed to pray, Brother Andrew says.

As if in answer, someone came out of the saint's house, we heard the footsteps, I felt a touch on my sleeve, pulling me along.

Just you, a voice said.

Together we walked up the hillside through the dead vineyard, towards a moonless sky, and in the darkness I recognised my silent shadow companion as Aude, my mountain girl.

Have you been true to me? she said.

In the starlight she could not have seen me blush.

I said that the town she had described to me in the mountains was not the one I had arrived at. She had told me about a languishing place.

The villagers grow rich on my sister, she said. They grow fat and she dwindles away.

And you?

I do what I can in the service of my sister. My sister says we do what we have to do. We have no choice in the face of God's will.

She sermoned me. She said that if we have no choice then there can be no sin, because there is no sin without freedom. And she told me that being without sin is like being without death.

These are some of the things she said; and she complained about the cupidity of the villagers and the sacrifice they were making of her sister, and the night was cold, and we walked beside each other, shoulders touching, and sometime she shivered, or maybe it was me.

And then she had to go. She took me to a stone lodge on the edge of the vineyard and told me that I and my companions could sleep there without disturbance.

I thanked her. I asked if I could see her the following day and she said that she only could see me at night, because she was too busy in service to her sister.

I asked if I might meet her sister but Aude laughed at me and said that she did not think I could afford the price.

I found Brother Andrew outside and Brother Bernard inside the house that serves as a tavern and I took them to the stone lodge in the vineyard. And in this way did our first night pass in the village of the living saint.

Saint Mary Magdalene's Day

Mary is called Magdalene, which is understood to mean, remaining guilty, or it means, armed, or, unconquered, or, magnificent. Before her conversion she remained in guilt, burdened with the debt of eternal punishment. In her conversion she was armed and rendered unconquerable by the armour of penance. After her conversion she was magnificent in the superabundance of grace, because where trespass had abounded, grace was superabundant.

There are some who say that Mary Magdalene was espoused to John the Evangelist, who was about to take her as his wife when Christ called him away from his nuptials, whereupon she, indignant at having been deprived of her spouse, gave herself up to every sort of voluptuousness. And there are those who allege that Christ honoured John with special evidences of his affection because he had taken him away from delight. These tales are to be considered false and frivolous.

She was well-born, out of noble stock, and very rich; and sensuous voluptuousness keeps company with riches. Renowned as she was for her beauty and her riches, she was no less known for the way she gave her body to lust – so much so that her proper name was forgotten and she was commonly called The Sinner. When Christ was preaching at the home of Simon the leper, the divine will directed her there. Being a sinner she did not dare mingle with the righteous, but stayed back and washed the Lord's feet with her tears, dried them with her hair, and anointed them with precious ointment.

This is the Magdalene upon whom Jesus conferred such great graces and to whom he showed so many marks of love. He cast seven devils out of her, set her totally afire with love of him, counted her among his closest familiars, was her guest, had her do the housekeeping on his travels, and kindly took her side at all times. He defended her when the Pharisee said she was unclean, when her sister implied that she was lazy, when Judas called her wasteful. Seeing her weep he could not contain his tears. For love of her he raised her brother Lazarus, four days dead, to life; for love of her he freed her sister Martha from the issue of blood she had suffered for seven years.

Fourteen years after the passion and accession of Our Lord, the Magdalene travelled to Marseille, where she converted many idolaters with her preaching, because all who heard her were in admiration of her beauty, her eloquence, and the sweetness of her message: the mouth which had pressed such pious and beautiful kisses on the Saviour's feet breathed forth the sweetness of the word of God so profusely.

Later, the blessed Mary Magdalene, wishing to devote herself to heavenly contemplation, retired to an empty wilderness, and lived unknown for thirty years in a place made ready by the hands of angels. There were no streams of water there, nor nourishment, nor the comfort of grass or trees. Every day at the seven canonical hours she was carried aloft by angels and with her bodily ears heard the glorious chants of celestial hosts.

After her own accession, many miracles attended: the dead were brought back to life; the blind made to see; prisoners were freed from their chains. One penitent, visiting her tomb, had the Magdalene appear to him as a lovely, sad-eyed woman supported by two angels, one on either side. The penitent soon felt so great an outpouring of grace in himself that he renounced the world, entered the religious life, and lived a very holy life thereafter. At his death, Mary Magdalene was seen standing with angels beside the bier, and she carried his soul, like a pure white dove, with songs of praise into heaven.

•

When we wake there is a pot of fresh water and a loaf of bread outside the doorway to our lodge. But today is a Friday, so we fast and spend the day in contemplation and prayer. Aude and I make a tryst on the hillside at night.

Her family's prosperity is restored. The villagers grow rich on her sister. They lost their relic, their church and land lie neglected, their income is far greater now than before.

The second time I see my Aude she talks far less of her sister, whose saintliness seems to be oppressive to her, and she talks less too of sin and will. Instead, she speaks, softly, as if to herself, as if it is accidental that I happen to be over-hearing her thoughts, of exile and escape.

The village holds its strange work at too bright a pitch, as if the high point of ecstasy that some music builds to, to celebrate the Almighty One in a hot deliverance, is being sung, and lived, perpetually.

My companions are impatient to leave this place. They find its ways irksome upon them. The saint is not permitted to us, we should proceed with our journey, they say. We still have far to go.

I make excuses, I reiterate our desire to receive a blessing from the saint. They accuse me of playing the part of a lover. They threaten to go on without me. You have been subject to another enchantment, they say.

And so I tell my Aude that we will have to go.

I am not stopping you from doing anything, she says.

She asks me, as she has before, What is your great sin? Why do you need absolution?

And I tell her that only a visit to her sister can restrain my companions from continuing on.

She was angry with me. She reminded me of something that she had said in the mountains, that I would prefer her sister to her, but I do not remember her having said that.

. . .

My Master teaches us to be careful with talk of miracles. In his Great Work, he writes,

If the experiment of the magnet in relation to iron were not known to the world, it would seem a great miracle.

Aude's brother led me into the house. The people outside were angry at my undeserved privilege of being taken directly into the house and into a small corner room, which was dimly lit by candles like an altar.

The saint was lying on a bed. Her body was narrow, her clothes dirty and torn. Her mother was combing her short hair.

The saint sent her mother away. The others who were in the room made as if they were conceding me an audience but they were listening most intently. Sometime one of them would be so brave as to touch me or even her while we were talking. One even dared to touch the wounds on her feet.

Have you been true to me? she said.

I might have blushed. I did not know her.

But she knew me. She asked me about my journey. She named my companions. She mentioned a donkey that I took as a judgement on our companion Bernard.

Our listeners, her devotees, praised her, her knowledge that God had given to her of life everywhere, even the lives of strangers.

She sent all the others away so I was alone with the saintly girl.

She asked me to sit a little away from her, because, in this very dim room, the light was too bright for her eyes. And then she asked me questions.

She asked me where I had come from, and why I was travelling and whether a great sin was the reason for my journey. I told her no, I had committed sins, but not great ones; that I was on a mission.

She asked me to tell her the nature of my mission, and the room seemed to expand and contract again, and I heard a great rushing in my ears, as if a sea were all around us.

I do not know if I can tell you, I said.

She asked if I had a lover, if my heart was promised to anyone, and I did not answer. She asked me what my opinion was of her sister, and which of them I did prefer; and again, I found reason not to answer.

The dimness of the room, the harshness of her voice as she led us in prayer.

When we had prayed, I asked for her blessing on our journey but she said that she could not give it because it would be ungodly for her to bless a journey whose purpose was being denied her; and she knew my name and those of my companions, and the names of some of the places we had come from; and she told me to visit her again the following day, and she said that she might be able to bless me then.

My companions are grieved that we did not receive a blessing from the saint. I tell them that I can hope for it to be delivered on the following day, and in this way, despite their impatience, I persuade them to stay here longer. They have given up hope of meeting the saint themselves, nor does this greatly worry them. They have no doubt of her sanctity but they are restless to move on.

When I meet Aude that evening she asks me my opinion

of her sister, and I tell her that she has made a great impression upon me. Aude finds reasons to chide me, she calls me a great hypocrite. We dispute and she is gone.

• • •

Again I meet with the saint, in her dimly lit room that smells of sanctity and blood.

The saint in her illness has become more than herself. Her soul can barely be contained in her fragile body and stretches out over geography and memory. She is like Brother Andrew, she is like my mother whom I never knew, she is like her sister, the mountain girl.

I have told her of our mission, my Master, and she has blessed it, even though it seems to have saddened her.

You are not alone, she tells me. There is another, a second messenger who carries a similar book. He travels faster than you.

She will not tell me any more, not even his name, nor his location, no matter how much I plead, no matter how my heart aches to hear that my Master has entrusted my mission to another, a rival, perhaps an enemy.

He travels alone, as will you, she says.

A night cloud departs and starlight pierces the room, almost bright enough to write by; it shines upon her cheekbones, the sweat on her brow, and she can no longer be what I would imagine her be, with her familiarity and her unknown, perhaps unknowable ways, and this is the moment of recognition when I see the game that is being played here, that there are no sisters, the saint and the servant, just one, whom I am more than a little scared by.

She says that she wishes to show me something.

She is looking sly and proud and shimmering beautiful, never so lovely or so strange – and what is it that she wishes to show me? What demands that I step so closely towards her, to go towards her outstretched arms, her eyes, her fingers? I suspect that it is something about me that she intends to show – a cause for shame or doubt, an exposure of something essential and wrong.

Look, she says. And she climbs off her bed to sit close to me by the fire, which casts wild figures on to her face, and she extends her arms towards me and I extend mine towards her, a tentative kind of answer, or protection.

Look, she says.

As if intent on displaying a secret treasure to share, she lifts her skirts and the starlight and the firelight cast pale wormy shadows over her skin, the too-narrow bones, the darker holes that have been gouged on the sides of her wrists and ankles.

This is the instrument that has caused my wounds, she says drawing out a long rusty nail from, it seems, the air.

And here, she says extending her arms again and rolling her hands to display the bleeding wounds on the underside of her wrists; another, she says and a second rusty nail appears that looks as aged as the Cross.

She closes her eyes; her body is not strong, the Passion is great. Her hands open, the nails fall to the floor.

I write this. My words spread across the page like rust and blood.

There are no sisters, there is one, playing two parts, and she is asking me which of them I prefer, as if the question has meaning, as if whichever I choose, so will she be.

When she is my mountain girl, she chafes at her servitude, she longs to be abroad and free. When she is playing the part of the saintly sister, she becomes her. I am convinced of her powers; she has become the part she plays.

She has made other prophecies. I shall reach my

destination, but I shall do it alone, and there I shall reach my death.

And darkness shall cover me; but darkness shall not be dark to you and night shall be light as the day.

Saint Apollinaris's Day

The saint's name is formed of the words *pollens*, which means powerful, and *ares*, meaning virtue: and Apollinaris was powerful in virtue. Or the name comes from *pollo*, which means admirable, and *naris*, by which discretion is understood; and it indicates a man of admirable discretion. Or the name is formed by *a*, which means without, *polluo*, which means pollute, and *ares*, which means virtue; and Apollinaris was a virtuous man who was unpolluted by vices.

My name is interpreted as grace of God, or one in whom is God's grace, or one to whom a gift is given, or to whom a particular grace is given by God. And how far have I fallen, and how much farther shall I fall.

Light has been extinguished. My companions walk so much faster than I, and wait for me to catch up. Walking is hard, writing almost impossible, even though my body has suffered no injury. I am invincible in prophecy, consumed by sadness.

I think of the gospel of Gottschalk that we heard in Paris. As in Aude's vision of the world as a place without freedom, it does not matter what we do; there is nothing that we may choose; there is no consequence. We are doomed to salvation or else doomed to hell; and the only thing that persists is the satisfaction of my Master's will. I must reach Viterbo before the second messenger. This, and all else, is God's to dispose.

． ． ．

We have found our way to a beautiful place, and this is how it happened, my lord, this is how we came here.

We were in a Ghibelline town. Everywhere, banners for the Emperor, scurrility to the Pope, his image drawn on the city walls. We walked uneasily, expecting at any time to be unmasked as men of the Pope.

And maybe we were not ready enough with our pretence of loyalty to the Germans. Maybe our sincerity glowed through, like gold shining beneath paint. In a narrow street, as evening was falling, doors shut against us, curious heads watching our pain with no thought of helping us, we were shoved, kicked, beaten from wall to wall, made sport of by a foul band of abusers. They took delight in watching us fall, in seeing our skin rubbed raw against the harsh stones of the houses they threw us against, in hearing the crack of the bone in Brother Andrew's arm. Our mildness counted against us. Our refusal to fight gave further fire to their rage, with blows and more kicks and blasphemous epithets. They did not understand that forbearance shames the aggressors and not the objects of their violence. And I knew they could not harm me because the saint's prophecy protects me, but I do not think it extends to Brother Bernard and poor Brother Andrew.

I interposed my body between our assailants and my companions and even if the prophecy were to fail, I was content to offer myself as a sacrifice. But this angered them further, as if they recognised the protection that watches over me, and they made no attempt to harm me but instead tried to find ways around me to hurt my beloved companions.

And then our oppressors were scattered in a storm of hooves. A horse reared above us, its eyes wild, like those of the men who had been assailing us, a frenzy of blood and forgetting. Its rider, our deliverer, settled his mount, pulled it to stand still. He regarded us, as we pulled our cloaks around our damaged bodies. Brother Andrew's beauty was unspoiled by the blood and the engorged skin swelling on his face. I wiped some of the blood away from my own face, but could feel that I was merely rubbing dirt into the wounds; and there was a voluptuousness in this; the dirt scratching and tearing at the lips of the wound brought me closer to Aude.

Our deliverer looked most intently at Bernard, who was standing, moody, unbroken. He said,

Why do you not fight back? You could fell an ox with a single blow.

It was getting dark, moonless, and I had thought at first our deliverer was a giant on horseback, a hero worthy of legend; but his voice was no deeper than a girl's and he was even younger than me.

I replied, saying,

We are not permitted to use violence. No Christian should.

Your companions? Are they fools?

They have little understanding of Italian. Only Latin.

The boy knight, whom I later discovered to be named Prince Guido, said,

It is the language of lawyers and clerics and knaves. Which are you?

I told him, to which he replied with scorn, saying,

What quality do the cleric and the cockerel share? They are the only beasts who feel no melancholy after fornication.

He seemed to take no gratification in this remark, but

neither did he acknowledge its obscenity. It was as if he was compelled to speak a necessary truth that he had learned at the table of his elders and thought it reflected well on him to share.

But you speak Italian. What grants you the gift of languages? The Devil?

This was not the place to tell him of my Master, of his pedagogic programme, of the quest for the Universal Grammar, to build the machine that would demolish the Tower of Babel.

And, in truth, this knight was a little like my Master. He was young, and knightly, but there was the same temper of disputatiousness. But my Master, you are more urgent and more final, the need to prove yourself and to make, so many projects, in so little time.

Come with me. We will clean your wounds.

And he led us through the town as the night fell, up a hill and to a castle.

My companions and I were placed in an upstairs room of the castle. I had lain in my bed imagining sleep to be impossible, despite my weariness, in this unaccustomed solitude, the wide dimensions of the room that held us. I have become used to sleep close to Brother Andrew, to hear his heartbeat, to feel it indivisible from my own, wake to Brother Bernard beside us cough and fart. And then I was so quickly asleep and for a great time, I think, until I was pierced awake by morning light, whereupon I lay in my bed, stilled by the silence, the great space around me, telling myself I would arise for my prayers when one of my companions should also rouse or when I should hear some sound from outside and then when I did hear women talking in the corridor, the voices of men outside my wall, I was made even more timid.

Finally the sounds of Brother Bernard waking came to me, heard through the distance that separated us, and that lifted me. I prayed, I thanked God for bringing us this deliverance, and I went to the window and looked down into the courtyard where a pair of soldiers were arguing about the feet of a horse and where a kitchen maid was drawing water from a well and where a hawk was rising from the glove of a boy, and I watched the hawk fly and I said aloud the words that God spoke to Job, Does the hawk wax feathered by your wisdom, spreading her wings to the south, or at least I began to say these words, which were full in my mind but stopped dead on my tongue when I saw the bird fly over the white battlements, which were cut at the top in the shape of a swallow's tail.

Brother Bernard came to the window and I showed him what I had seen. My dread multiplied in the duration it took for his eyes to take in the shape of the battlements and for this image to travel into an understanding.

We waited in our room. We grew hungry. We prayed. We took turns to empty our bowels into a pot, the contents of which Brother Bernard threw out of the window. Perhaps this is what alerted a serving man in the company of our deliverer to fetch us.

He brought us into a grand hall with banners unfurled along its sides and long tables weighed down with immense quantities of food, the roasted carcasses of birds and beasts, rare fruits, white loaves of bread. He stopped Brother Bernard, whose hunger is larger than his fear, from reaching to tear a grape off its vine. We were instructed to wait at the back of the hall, to one side, and we watched as the hall filled, our deliverer's party on one side, the host's on the other, a table at the centre, where our deliverer, the haughty prince, sat between his father to his right, and a fearful girl, whose tremors and fear spoke for our own. Our deliverer is named Prince Guido, he is the son of Cavalcante de Cavalcanti, who is a great lord, who carries himself with measure and a solemnity that does not exclude the possibility of mirth. Cavalcante de Cavalcanti is a Guelph, contracting an alliance with his enemies through the agency of the body of his son. Prince Guido looked weary throughout the ceremony. His future bride is even younger than he is, and timorous, and shivered any time a word or even a look was directed towards her.

Prince Guido's father made a speech, and the girl's father made a speech, and we were standing at the back of the hall, behind the tables of the Cavalcantis, and could barely hear any of it under the roar and complaints of our empty bellies.

Brother Bernard was impressed by the grandeur of the occasion, the riches on display, the table in the centre of the room where gifts had been laid out, the grand costumes and silks and jewels, a cardinal splendid in red.

And Brother Andrew too, protecting his injured eye against the light and colour and ceremony, he asked me what it was that was taking place, and I told him that it was a betrothal party, our haughty prince Guido was being transacted in future marriage to the shy shivering girl, of whom no signs of womanliness could be detected. And I said that we had to speak to the cardinal, find our way into his party; because he was on the Guelph side of the room and would be returning home after the ceremony no doubt to his master the Pope.

They talked interminably, of the honour of their families, of the future union, of strife affecting Italy, which could be healed, the harmony of the country embodied in the betrothed couple. Prince Guido hardly ever looked at his bride, Beatrice Uberti, and he lost his haughtiness only when his father spoke to him, whereupon he became properly respectful.

Several times I tried to move towards the cardinal as he ate, but each time I was held back by one of the servants. We were exhorted to eat, to delight in this incorporation of peace, but we were not permitted to move from our station.

Belligerent looks passed between the Cavalcantis and the Ubertis. Young men of both sides hardly ate, kept their attention fixed on the movements of their supposed new allies, their brothers; and it was because of this that the ranks of either side were not to be broken, and it was because of this that we were not permitted to move, that I was not permitted to approach the cardinal, who was one of the first guests to leave, and when he did, it was with a great move-ment of farewells and kisses and the sound of horses outside and much bowing; and our opportunity had passed in which we might find safe passage through this territory of Ghibellines, when we might gain speed on our journey to his holiness the Pope, when we might gain time and distance on the second messenger.

Instead, we were invited to ride back to the castle of our deliverers in the cart that brought the presents for the bride-to-be and her Ghibelline family.

We rode to Cavalcante's castle in the cart, delighted by the unaccustomed speed, hardly noticing the pain in our bodies when the cart rocked or jolted our injuries.

When we arrived at the castle, we were assigned a room even more sumptuous than the one the previous night, which has confirmed Brother Bernard in his view that the Guelphs are in every way superior to the Ghibellines.

And now, we wear other people's clothes, voluptuous. We sleep on silken beds in rooms scented with rose water. And this is how it happened, my lord, this is how we came here, to this castle of white towers that shimmer in a moonless night, a place that might have been wished for in a dream.

Saint Christina's Day

Christina, the devout, in a pagan household, smashed her father's idols and distributed the gold and silver to the poor. Her father ordered her to be stripped and beaten by twelve men until they fell down from exhaustion. Then he had her bound in chains and thrown into prison. When she refused to worship the pagan gods, her father ordered her flesh to be torn off with hooks and her tender limbs broken; and Christina picked up pieces of her flesh and threw them in her father's face, saying, Take that, tyrant! and eat the flesh you begot!

Then her father ordered her to be stretched on a wheel and a fire of oil was lighted beneath her but the flames leapt out and killed fifteen hundred men. When it was night, her father ordered his henchmen to tie a large stone around her neck and throw her into the sea. But Christ himself came to save her, and baptise her, and commended her to the care of the archangel Michael, who led her ashore.

Her father died that very night, but a wicked judge who was called Elius succeeded him. Elius had an iron cradle prepared and fired with oil, pitch and resin. Christina was thrown into this cradle and four men were ordered to rock it back and forth so she might burn more quickly. But Christina praised God, who willed that she be rocked in the cradle like a newborn babe. The judge, angrier than ever, had her head shaved and ordered her to be led naked through the city to the temple of Apollo. But she directed a command to the idol, which collapsed into dust; and the hateful judge was stricken with fear and expired.

His successor had Christina thrown into a furnace. There, for five days, she walked about, singing with angels, and was unharmed. The judge Julianus had two asps, two vipers and two cobras put in with her; but the vipers licked her feet, the asps clung to her breasts without hurting her, and the cobras wrapped themselves around her neck and licked her sweat.

Now Julianus had Christina's breasts cut off, and milk flowed from them instead of blood. Lastly, he had her tongue cut out, but she, never losing the power of speech, threw the severed tongue in Julianus's face, blinding him in the eye. Goaded to wrath, Julianus shot two arrows into her heart and one into her side, and she, pierced through and through, breathed forth her spirit to God. These events occurred in about the year 287, in the vicinity of Bolsena.

My preaching does not attract an audience. I have learned, when meeting with indifference, to concentrate on blood and suffering. People like to hear the agonies of the martyrs. Brothers Andrew and Bernard make their amens, Brother Bernard goes around the few people listening to us in the courtyard but they just look scornful and go on their way and Brother Bernard's hand is empty. The only ones left are a mother and her distressed child, who makes sharp intermittent shrieks like an idiot imitating a crow and holds himself.

You are wise, the mother says to me.

Not really, I say but Brother Bernard does not agree; seeing a possible advantage, he tells the poor woman that I am very wise.

Maybe you can heal my son.

I do not know if I can heal your son.

Please heal my son.

She tells me that he has not been able to empty his bladder in days. He is in pain, his idiot shrieks announce this. He holds his little penis and shakes it like a favourite pet who has inexplicably died.

I tell her to wait in the courtyard, and I tell Brother Andrew to borrow some wine from the castle, and I go up the stairs into our corner room that's built into the wall. I bring back the powdered root of iris that Father Gabriel gave me, and I mix it in the wine that Brother Andrew has brought in the proportions that my Master showed me when he was suffering from a similar malady.

The boy does not wish to drink. He moves his head from side to side to avoid the remedy. The liquid splashes on to his chin, his tunic, the hands of his mother who is squeezing his nose tight with one hand and pulling his jaws open with the other. People going about their work look at us as if we could have provided a better spectacle.

The boy shrieks, vomits, is made to drink some more, and shrieks again. His mother spits three times, and leads him away. I gather up my utensils, the pot, the wine, the mixing stick.

The lord Cavalcante de Cavalcanti came into the courtyard with his son. He was displeased. He said,

Why do you beg when everything is provided? You are here as our guests. You do not need to beg. It is dishonouring, for all of us.

I had no reply to make other than shame. Brother Andrew bowed, and returned the remainder of the wine to the store.

Prince Guido said,

They are typical friars and this is what friars do. Try to frighten our people with their stories and drink our wine and ask for money. I should have left them to the mercies of their enemies.

I said,

It is not like that.

How then is it? said the great lord Cavalcante de Cavalcanti.

I was sorry to have grieved them. His spirit is unruly, like his son's, but it is tempered with wisdom and due care. He is a father to his people, a host to us, and I could see the picture that had been made, to our discredit.

I said,

We will be on our way. Thank you for all that you have given us.

Our manners had failed to match their hospitality. But, I reflected, it was no bad thing, to be on our way. Our injuries were healing, our bellies were full. It was good to have been met with kindness, but we had a mission to fulfil and somewhere out there the second messenger was making his progress to Viterbo.

The lord and his son were turning away from us; we were becoming vapour in their minds, vanishing from their memories, when the boy we had seen returned into the courtyard running ahead of his mother. His tunic was wetter than before, both were joyful. The mother bowed, she made her son kiss my hand. She talked of the Flood, she marvelled at the quantity of urine that her son had been able to expel. Again she bowed before me.

We became solid again in the notice of the lord Cavalcante de Cavalcanti. He made the mother account for her behaviour. He asked her for a full description of what had been transacted between us and then he turned again to me, asking me to explain the means of my remedy, and the basis for it in my knowledge and experience.

I told him something of my education, I praised my Master. I told Cavalcante de Cavalcanti that I was an unworthy vessel for the wisdom of the most learned man in Christendom. And the lord asked me if I accepted that I was under an obligation to him and his house and when I admitted that I was, he said that there would be no more talk of us leaving, and he said,

You shall heal the sick of the castle. And you shall educate my son.

I protested. I said that my time was not my own, that I was on a mission directed by my Master, but the lord is accustomed to getting his way, and he made me agree that our injuries are such that our progress would be impeded, and he promised satisfactory occupations for my companions, according to their capacities, and he made me consent that I would do as he asked while we gathered our full strength, and that I would proceed to do as he asked until our bodies were healed, or if my cures met with no effect, or until his son had grown weary of my instruction as he had of all his previous masters, and whichever of these should occur first then our covenant should end with no ill-feeling or bad-usage on either side.

• • •

Cavalcante de Cavalcanti promised us apt occupations. Mine are twofold: to instruct the prince, although I am not sure that my knowledge is being transmitted, and I do not have the means to enforce it with slaps and blows; and to minister to the sick of the castle. I have found a joy in healing people, and a joy too in satisfying a curiosity about the doings and failings of human hearts and bodies.

A servant girl has been assigned to help me because otherwise the people are too many outside the room I work in. The room is built into a corner of the castle walls with a staircase leading up to it, a skylight, and a door set into the darker recesses. I keep my medicines in a cupboard by the door, where the heat does not reach. Knights from the castle, and their ladies, and serving girls and serving boys, and grooms from the stables, and old women, whose characters have been made indistinct by their great age, and men who work in the kitchen and men who work on the land, and milkmaids and ostlers and administrators all come to see me, filling the courtyard outside my door all the way to the well.

Their rank determines their precedence. A stable boy, who has been waiting from nones to vespers, whose face is inflamed and pitted with the malady that afflicts him, who has nearly reached my room on several occasions, only to be thrust further away each time by the needs of a superior, is finally on the threshold again when his master, the great lord himself, thrusts past him and into my receiving room and shuts the door behind him.

The lord has an energy that will not abate. The eagle flies and then rests, the horse sleeps in his stable, the lord Cavalcante is seldom still. He walks around my room, he picks up handfuls of chamomile and asks,

What is this for? Which of my people needs this?

And I am answering, telling him that I had decocted the herb in wine to administer to the troublesome spleen of his commander of guards and I would have gone on to describe the process whereby I had intended to mix it in honey to apply to the face of the stable boy, but Cavalcante de Cavalcanti is already on the move, the chamomile scattered behind him, a bowl of celery-leaved buttercup in wine now spilling over his hands, which are out of character with the rest of him, so pale and slender, fingers that should be picking at the strings of an instrument or pressed together in prayer, and then he is walking on again, to my pot of parsnip roots and wild orchid candied with honey and dates, and asking for its purpose and its intended recipient and I wonder if I should tell him that it is the daughter of the chamberlain who asked for this, heartsick with love for the son of her lord, and that she had asked me too for a stratagem to go along with it, like the commander of an army seeking help from a foreign general, she should give it to him how? and she should give it to him when? and how is she to make sure that after Guido ingests it hers is the first face that he will see? – but the father of the object of her idolatry is again on the move, and I consider that maybe the chamberlain's daughter loves the son rather than his father because Cavalcante is so high above her, just as it is easier to love Jesus than it is to love God, because Jesus is human, half of him is human – until he sits finally, in the chair that my visitors use, and the girl who helps me is about to enter with a fresh pot of vinegar, but leaves again when she sees who is with me and I do not know if her consternation indicates that she suffers from a similar malady to the chamberlain's daughter or to the other young women I have seen who have asked for something that should be forbidden but which I have been persuaded, after threats and blandishments and tears – it is tears that persuade me, I am always moved by tears – to give them, the mixture that takes many ingredients to combine, and time too to enable the combination, to stifle the life that grows inside them.

Cavalcante sits in the chair, one of his legs over its side, his back twisted, his neck crooked, as if only with the bonds of discomfort might his unruly spirit be compelled to be still.

The serving girl is like Aude, but not in any particularity.

And Cavalcante says,

How would you cure the ill that afflicts me?

I answer that first I would require it to be named and then I could go to my store and find the elements of its remedy. I have grown confident in my powers, aided by a medicine of my own, my Master's wisdom combined with that of Father Gabriel's.

And what is this? the lord says.

He opens the strings that tie a small muslin bag, in which I have stored the plant I found in the mountains, its seeds and black root and folded leaves, its white petals.

I am honest with him. I can think of no reason not to be. I tell him that this is the plant I have discovered, whose powers I can only conjecture.

He asks about the source of the power and he asks how the plant will operate on the human body, and I have to admit that I do not know. I do not tell him my secret hope, that this is the plant called moly, that Hermes gave to Odysseus to protect him from Circe's magic, grown from blood, the elixir of healing, dangerous for mortal men to tear out from the soil, but not for the gods. Because that is something for my Master and the lesson I have already learned is that one man may not serve two Masters. So I quote from another part of Homer, telling Lord Cavalcante that I wonder if it is the drug that Helen, the daughter of Zeus, administered to enable men to forget their troubles.

A drink of this, once mixed in with wine, would prevent

any man from letting a tear fall on his cheek for one whole day, not even if his mother and his father died, or if, in his own presence, men armed with swords hacked down his brother or his son, as he looked on.

The son, Guido, haughty, impetuous, perhaps the smaller mirror of his father, arrives to tell me that we are due for today's lesson. And if he is the mirror of his father, he is also, although this might be self-flattery, the mirror of his unworthy instructor, because this is how I was with my own Master, impatient for his wisdom, his presence.

My helper returns after her lord and the prince have gone. She puts the vinegar on a shelf with an act of ease that I choose not to question. She grinds down the rocket seeds, which indeed is the work I would have chosen for her but she is doing it without instruction, as if she has already heard my thoughts, and this could well be so, because I have heard hers, which plead with me not to ask her about her feelings towards her young lord.

Guido is an avaricious learner, who drives his unworthy teacher to the limits of his knowledge. He asks me about the transmission of objects to the senses, and I tell him about the tremors that accompany sound and odour, and I describe the passage of light, its scintillation. I refer him to Ptolemy's second book on Optics, to the third book by Alhazen, to Aristotle on perspective, and to the summit of this, the *Opus Majus* of Roger Bacon.

We talk of the nature of light, the powers of vision that receive the universal species cast by the perceived objects. I tell him of the tremble of reception on the humours of the eyes, and I do not know if any of this has been transmitted, because Guido moves restlessly as I talk, and when the lesson is over, the teacher is more exhausted than his pupil.

• • •

Saint Christopher's Day

Before Christopher was baptised, he was called Reprobus, meaning outcast, but afterwards he was called Christophoros, the Christ-bearer. On account of his immense size and strength he was welcomed wherever he might choose to roam and at whichever court of power he might choose to ally himself with. Reprobus had found his way to the court of a king who had the largest army in Canaan. But when he saw the king look fearful and make the sign of the cross on his forehead when his jester made mention of the Devil, and the king admitted that he feared the Devil above all, Reprobus grieved at the limits of the king's power and left the Canaanite court in search of the Devil to accept him as his master.

In the desert, he came across a great host of soldiers, and at its head was one more fierce and more terrible than the rest. This was the Devil, whom Reprobus accepted as his lord and master. They marched along the highway until they came to a cross erected at a roadside. When the Devil saw it, he left the road and led his men over a wild and desolate tract before returning to the road. Reprobus made the Devil tell him why he was so frightened of the cross, and when he heard that there was a man named Christ who was nailed to a cross, and that whenever the Devil saw the sign of the cross, he was filled with terror and ran away, Reprobus who was becoming Christopher said, Well then, this Christ, whose sign you dread so much, is greater and more powerful than you. Therefore I am leaving you and going in search of the greater prince.

My full strength is returning, and my store of medicines is becoming depleted, and I should go before I have too few treasures to return to my Master. The lord Cavalcante still will not confess the malady that ails him.

Brother Bernard works in the forge, beating metal in the fire. He has a cloth belted at his waist that covers most of his lower body. His chest is bare. Sweat and smut and fire. He has learned to craft jewellery for the women of the castle, and sometime he will hide brooches or rings still warm beneath the folds of his cloak.

Brother Andrew, who was the most injured of us, has no occupation. He swims in the river, he passes time on land with a serving girl of the kitchen, who tends his wounds.

I have position here. People call me lord. As does my helper, who has hair as red as Tuscan earth and moves with a lightness that suggests she is at any time about to dance; but she does not dance, and I do not hold her, even though there is something in me that impels me to, and an answering feeling in her that requires me to.

Cavalcante de Cavalcanti asks me if I am still so eager to leave his castle. I tell him it is an honourable and harmonious place. But yes, I tell him. I must leave.

The head dictates to the body. Cavalcante de Cavalcanti, despite his appetites and turbulence, is a wise ruler.

Stay until the feast, the lord tells me. This will be a night for pleasure, not like one of those interminable Ghibelline affairs with lengthy speeches and everyone trying to work out how soon they might be able to leave without causing too much offence.

Cavalcante de Cavalcanti believes in pleasure. He says,

We all desire the same things. I wish for what the lowliest peasant desires. Food in my belly, a warm place to sleep, beautiful objects to gaze upon, and a pretty girl on the end of my screw.

Where does God come into this?

Why nowhere of course.

He is a follower of Epicurus and Lucretius. The body dies, nothing persists. The world he lives in is empty of spirit, no matter how harmonious its order. This, I am sure, is the malady that afflicts him. And one I do not have the remedy for.

My pupil apologised for his father,

My father likes to startle people. Particularly if he has a fondness for them. But sometime I think that he believes what he says.

Later, when I was with my companions, I asked Brother Bernard how many gems he has stolen.

He said that he had not counted, he said that he could not have stolen them; because if everything is free there can be no theft. This made me wonder where Cavalcante draws his income from. No trade goes on with other castles or towns. And yet, all here is in surfeit.

I said,

I think they are heretics.

Brother Andrew replied,

I think we are all heretics.

Brother Andrew is the true Franciscan. If God is everywhere why then do we have to remove ourselves from Him? The true worship is in the fields and streams and on the body of another of his creatures. I will be true to Aude.

I have already been here too long.

Saint Anna's Day

Anna, of Bethlehem, is said to have had three husbands, Joachim, Cleophas and Salome. Joachim, a Galilean from the town of Nazareth, was her first husband. They were both righteous and walked without reproach in the commandments of the Lord. They divided all their goods, one part being reserved for the temple and its ministers, the second for transient strangers, and the third part for their own needs. They lived for twenty years without offspring and made a vow to the Lord that if He gave him a child, they would dedicate it in service to God. And she gave birth to one daughter, Mary, whom she gave in marriage to Joseph, and who brought forth Christ the Lord. Joachim died and Anna married Cleophas, Joseph's brother, and of him she had another daughter, whom she likewise named Mary, and who was married to Alpheus. This Mary bore her husband four sons, namely, James the Less, Joseph the Just also called Barsabas, Simon, and Jude. After the death of her second husband, Anna took a third, namely, Salome, of whom she had another daughter, whom she also called Mary and whom she gave as wife to Zebedee. This Mary had two sons by her husband, namely, James the Greater and John the Evangelist.

There were dining tables in the courtyard, dining tables in the great hall of the castle. Nearby villagers climbed the hill to the castle gates, where I stood with Guido and a pair of his men. Brothers Bernard and Andrew were elsewhere. I hardly ever see Brothers Bernard and Andrew. Guido and his men were guarding the passage in case any Ghibellines arrived uninvited to the feast.

My pupil Guido's mother died giving birth. This was fifteen years ago. His father has never remarried. Cavalcante de Cavalcanti is richer than he needs to be, and in this pagan Epicurean realm, he takes whichever woman he desires. I wonder how many of my pupil's half-brothers and -sisters there are in the castle.

147

It will not be dreary, Cavalcante promised. And it was not dreary. There was wine and roasted boar and roasted deer and lights hung inside different-coloured globes of glass that moved in the breeze and scattered blue and yellow and orange and green hues over the feasters. And there was smoke from the kitchen mixing in with the odour of roasted meat and the sweetness of the wine, and there were musicians from Brittany and dancers from Cadiz. In the hall there were discussions, held without rancour or discord. By the fountain there was song.

I saw Brother Bernard with the singers, his mouth open in joy, a pot of wine in his hand, his cloak open at his chest that was still smeared with smut from the forge. Brother Andrew was with the dancers, two girls from Cadiz who were showing him how to make the steps and turn.

All the Guelph lords of the region were here, with their chamberlains and retinues. And as well as all those manners of people, there are many more, whose intentions and trades I can only conjecture, and among them are emissaries from the Papal court, to whom I should announce myself and my mission, but from whom I have hid, despite the urgings of my companions, to whom I have been unable to give a reason why, because I cannot provide one to myself.

A Jew sits in the library to discuss finance with a cardinal of Rome and a Venetian banker. The Jew's appearance surprises me. I had been expecting something magical and monstrous. To mark out his tribe, he wears a Phrygian cap, which has a stiff round yellow base that covers his scalp and rises to a cone, and were it not for this, and the red robes of the cardinal, I should not have known him to distinguish him from the men he talks to.

Perhaps, I said to Andrew, a unicorn is just a horse with a Phrygian cap.

And then I retreated to a corner by the castle wall to pray and make penance for making the sort of sentence that sparkles and which would win me distinction, instead of making myself closer to God.

I talked with a learned man from Florence, and a dancing master from Cadiz. My helper sat beside me. There was no separation between the men and women in this ideal kingdom where all was celebration, and it felt as if this was the natural order of things, and everything else, the works and transactions of days that were not devoted to delight and feasting were just the negligible moments in between, like the passages of sleep where there is no dream.

The riches of Cavalcante de Cavalcanti seem endless, like King Solomon's, the jewels taken by Brother Bernard, the feasting, the hospitality, the rare books in the library; but there is no evidence of trade: the jewels produced in the forge are for the delight and adornment of the castle ladies. The learned man from Florence explained it to me. Cavalcante is a moneylender. He finances other men's courts, he lends money for wars; all the great men of Italy are in debt to him, pay the interest and accrual on his loans, even the Pope.

Beauty can never be usury's child.

And, I am saving this to the last, there is one grave company of men, which sits apart from everyone else.

These men are shortly to journey to Venice from where they will travel to the east; but one of their company has fallen sick in the swamplands of Sarzana.

They will be making nine Investigations of the people they encounter, the first regarding their origins, second their beliefs, third their rituals of worship, fourth their ways of living, fifth their strength, sixth their population, seventh their intentions, eighth their observance of laws and ninth their reception of envoys.

And they will be looking for elephants and unicorns, men with lions' manes, pillars of fire, strange bodies of water, flying machines, the marvellous monsters that live in seas and mountains and forests, the dog-headed people and the horse-footed people that Pliny wrote about, the celibate Ethiopians, dogs of such size the traveller told us about in the friary that can kill lions and pull down bulls, which are hitched by farmers to ploughs and warriors to their chariots.

It is being done for glory, and for God, and curiosity, and discovery, and commerce, and diplomacy, and simple adventure, which, I think, is what lures these men upon their expedition.

They have a clothier, who will adapt their dress to avoid causing offence to the people they travel amongst. And they have soldiers, to protect them. And they have merchants and bankers among them, or at least the sons of merchants and bankers. But they do not have a translator, because he is the one who fell sick in Sarzana.

Paradise is in the east, the Garden of Eden. The lost tribes of Israel are wandering the deserts of the east, and Alexander's Gate, behind which were locked up Gog and Magog, who feast on human flesh, is open, whether through might or earthquake or the dilapidation of age is unknown, and the Tartars are from the lands behind the Gate.

What do you know of them? I was asked by a member of the company.

They are a warlike, brutal and Godless people who roam a place of splendour.

Can you speak their language?

I could easily learn it. My Master has taught me the secrets of grammar.

We are going to the lands of the Tartars, they say, but we need someone to understand their language.

The traveller had cast a kind of sigaldry on all those who heard him. Even my Master envied him his experiences. I go further than him, my Master said. His studies sent his mind farther than China, but all the same he was envious. As the traveller said, But as God gives us the different fingers of the hand, so he gives to man different ways.

How I admired him, how I longed to be him; and this is the opportunity that I might become him, that I would bring back news from other places, see the great sights, and the monsters, the sheets of ice in the north, the route in the south where the sailors navigate with the sun on their right, that I would travel to the great men of learning in the great places of the world, no longer a messenger but someone to whom all doors are open. And I could persuade myself that this would not be a desertion, but a further extension of my Master's will, to whom I could return with accounts of far places and more rue, and coral, and the saffron that grows so plentifully behind Alexander's gates, to replenish the stock of treasures I have expended at Cavalcante's.

I may not, I said.

What of your companions? The giant.

He has no skill for languages.

How about the one who is dancing?

He is very fragile. He would quickly follow your companion of Sarzana.

And in this way, I resisted the temptation to join their expedition, and I protected Brothers Andrew and Bernard.

The musicians and dancers stood to the side, and the young men of the castle took turns to prove their prowess with rhyme. Their verses were intricate and skilled, like prayers or hymns. But even the Poet in Paris, the Crow, took delight in blaspheming. Here, it was as if He did not exist, they hardly glance His way with their verses about love, always love.

And then, the last to perform, Prince Guido. He takes his place, lit by candles, at the side of the room, approaching it with reluctance, as if it is against his will to be the cause of attraction. His father breaks off his conversation to attend to the words of his son. All the young women, except my helper, lean forward too. He clears his throat, he rubs at his hair, which is black, like his clothes. He looks at his boots as the first words come from his mouth as if unbidden.

He recites his first poem with diffidence and uncertain power, so the meaning of the whole becomes obscured by the phrases he abruptly charges with fire. He professes to be low in love, abashed before his heart's desire, abased before his love's cruel neglect – although his proud aspect and the attitude of the young women listening to him belie his words. It was the same sort of poem that the men before him had given, and skilled in its design of rhyme and shape, and when it is over, his last words followed by a silence that signifies its end, the other poets beat their thighs and the tables to lead the applause and announce their approval, but it was done as if to reward a clever child, who was not yet worthy of jealousy or fear.

His second subject is also to do with love. It is much more intricate in its construction than the first, and the sentences, always musical, turn in on themselves and wrap themselves around their predecessors and successors, while throughout an argument is advanced with a logic that is furthered by the patterns and rhymes and rhythms of the words with which it is made. The poem's subject and much of its diction have been taken from a previous lesson of ours, and I was wrong to have doubted the capacities of my student, because he has taken the stuff of philosophy and translated it from Latin to Italian and proved it with poetry.

Chi è questa che vèn, ch'ognom la mira,
Che fa tremar di chiaritate l'àre?

• • •

My companions have sought to persuade me that we must remain here. Three more days, Bernard said.

Tomorrow, I said.

Two more days, Andrew said.

Tomorrow, I said. Tomorrow morning I will be on my way. The second messenger is already in Italy.

Then there is less need for us to deliver the Book.

They speak so lightly, as if our mission were not sacred.

Bernard said,

The Ghibellines are looking for three of us. You will be safer on your own.

And Andrew said,

We are more noticeable. You speak their language. You can become one of a multitude in a way that we can not.

Whether these arguments are true or not, something has happened which is greater than our mission and our companionship.

Or you could stay here too. The second messenger may reach the Pope ahead of us anyway. There is a place for you here as there is for us.

I could fall. I could be tempted and fall. But wine may turn to vinegar and never back again.

Saint Pantaleon's Day

Before his conversion the young Pantaleon studied medicine with such effect that the Emperor Maximian appointed him his physician. One day as the future saint was discoursing with a holy priest named Hermolaus, the latter, after praising the study of medicine, concluded thus,

But, my friend, of what use are all your acquirements in this art, since you are ignorant of the science of salvation?

I stood at the gateway with my burden. The gate had been opened, the day stretched out wide below me, I laboured to carry my packages. The lord and his prince came quietly, maybe sorrowfully, to say farewell. My helper stood behind them. The lord Cavalcante offered me a horse to take for my journey, which I refused; and then a donkey to carry my load, which I accepted. Prince Guido made a great show of his skill at tying my packages to the back of the donkey.

I was not expecting my companions, because Aude had told me that I would reach my destination alone; but I waited for them nonetheless. And then Brother Andrew came into the courtyard. He was weeping as he stood beside me. I made to kiss him, but he had not come to make a parting. In his goodness, his loyalty, his simplicity, he was joining me for the journey. I then wept, and I did hold him, and I think the lord and the prince might have wept a little also.

We waited to see if Brother Bernard was going to join us, or say farewell, but the sun was rising, and we made our prayers, and received a benediction for our journey from the lord Cavalcante de Cavalcanti, and Brother Bernard still did not come, and we set off.

When we passed through the castle gateway, the donkey stopped walking. He put his head down, dug his feet into the loose stones of the castle approach, and refused to move. I pulled him at the head, Brother Andrew drove him from the rear. He still refused to walk, but in this manner we drove him through the loose stones down the slope.

And when we were down the hill, the donkey consented finally to walk, without, it seemed, ill feeling, as if our earlier battle had never occurred. We named him Bernard, because he was not so dissimilar from the member of the party that he had replaced. He talks as little, he shows a similar moodiness and strength.

Our way south had been described to us. After descending the hill from the castle, we took a path along a white road through a parched vineyard. The sun beat down on us and as we proceeded in the open, Brother Andrew grew afraid. Ahead of us the road of white stones proceeded through dry fields with hills ahead and behind. A bird of prey circled us. We had become heedless in the castle of our deliverers. Without their protection, we were once again exposed to the threat of the Ghibellines. I admonished Brother Andrew that God had protected us thus far, that at every moment when hope had seemed lost, fortune had interceded, and there was no reason to think that He would not always smile upon our journey, which is a righteous one.

Bernard the donkey released ordure as he walked.

It was good there, Brother Andrew said.

I told him that it was a place founded upon usury. I told him too that it was a place that had turned its back on God. I do not know if I persuaded either of us. I have not told him about Aude's prophecy.

•

Despite his similarities in character, the donkey Bernard is a poor substitute for our lost companion. The subtraction of one from the original three makes us less than two.

Brother Andrew for once is unmerry. He misses the castle, the pagan life. I point out trees, birds in trees, and he is withdrawn, offering no response as he proceeds on his way, one hand on the neck of Bernard the donkey. Even the sight of a stream wide enough to swim in fails to rouse Brother Andrew from his torpor.

And yet, I am merry to resume our journey. Colours seem brighter than before. The edges of things shimmer. It is as if I have my eyes wide open for the first time.

These are some of the things I saw: olive trees spreading their branches high to catch the sun and the rain, the hair on Bernard the donkey, rough and brown and so well-suited to him, which sometime I rubbed and he seemed to like it, particularly when I scratched hard at the thinner hair between his ears, which grew a little longer and sparser around the hard bumps of his scalp, the clouds passing about the sky, thin and narrow like sleeping men, their arms stretched out wide, like swimmers, or tucked beneath their chin, men who still dreamed of their mothers' cradle songs, and this was a game that we had been accustomed sometime to play, at which Brother Bernard, if he were to be roused, was always our master, because my imagination is a weak instrument and Andrew in his simplicity sees things as they are.

Andrew walks with his eyes on the path ahead. I drive us on, so much time has been spent away from the road, the Pope is waiting, the second messenger is ahead of us. I take care to walk ahead of my brother and in this way hope for the prophecy that protects me to protect him too.

Our enemies are everywhere. We hide in woods, in ditches by the side of roads, behind the walls of great castles. We may not go into towns in case that draws attention to ourselves and our load. Bernard the donkey does not like strangers. He has become unthankfully accustomed to me and Andrew. Any other man annoys him, provokes his fear, and anger, because inside his heart these two emotions act like one. Any stranger, a cleric, a soldier, a beggar, comes towards us and Bernard's long ears lie flat back on his head, his eyes narrow, his load shifts on his back as he prepares to kick and shriek.

This at least stirs Brother Andrew. He strokes Bernard's head, the softer, whiter hair on the insides of his ears, he whispers to him. Sometime he looks behind us, as if he could still see Cavalcante's castle.

Saint Martha's Day

Martha, sister of Mary Magdalene, who served, sister of Lazarus, who died and was raised, was Christ's hostess. She waited on the Lord and desired her sister to do likewise, because the whole world would not be enough to serve such a guest. As it is said, They made him a supper there, and Martha served.

We are learning husbandry. For the sake of the journey, we must tend to Bernard the donkey before we may look after ourselves. Bernard must drink before we drink, he must be fed before we may prepare our food, his resting place for the night is allocated before we can find ourselves a bed. We are like Martha, who served, and Mary, who served, of whom Judas Iscariot asked, Why should you spend money on oil to anoint His feet, when you might give it as charity to the poor?

There are hostel-keepers that turn away a donkey, without seeing him as the descendant of the noble beast who bore Our Lord into Jerusalem; and in truth Bernard is much depraved, a low contrarious descendant of Our Lord's bearer, hardly resembling of him, and revealing few signs of nobility. He is mean-tempered and sour in his service to us. When we feed him he takes the opportunity to bite our fingers, and poor Brother Andrew has fresh injuries to his hands.

The sun had fallen on our journey and come close to rising once more. Even before we reached this hospice, we had been turned away from others like it. Because our load was being carried rather than shared, we had walked farther than we were used to. Brother Andrew arrived in his perpetual downcast, Bernard the donkey in typical ill temper, making us wish for his predecessor. A quarter-moon was hanging low in a lightening sky, and I had been cheerful throughout our journey, as if there is a portion of good spirits to be shared, and I was carrying Andrew's.

As if in answer to my spirits, a kindly Dominican offered to feed Bernard and share his stable with him. Brother Andrew and I, our load renewed, entered the hospice.

It was like being returned to the malicious company of Simeon the Palmer and his men. They were pilgrims and merchants and clerics, sprawled around the room as they estimated the new arrivals, and our goods. And there were men who used to be soldiers, who lay in lassitude from the concussion of the nerves that my Master has observed soldiers suffer from in the aftermath of war. We found a place not so far from the door, where we sat by the wall, with our possessions between us, our arms over them.

We should have learned by now the lesson taught to us long ago in our journey by Master Roger, that the best way to hide something precious is to seem not to be hiding it at all.

And so it came to pass, my Master, as you would have supposed it would, hands and eyes upon us, a pressing of bodies and foul costume, from somewhere safe in his stable, I could hear the braying of Bernard in sorrow or sympathy, and Brother Andrew was fighting to protect your Book, my Lord.

This journey has been so long, and I have learned so little, and have proved myself only in unworthiness, but my mind was clear and I knew that no harm could befall me, because Aude's prophecy protects me, and while the battle was proceeding, I gathered the instruments I needed and then I shouted, loud, as if in that moment I owned the chest and breath of our lost companion. I made the announcement that we were men of great power, that we were the Pope's Friars whose legend had flown faster than the eagle. And when I saw that I had them, in various attitudes of curiosity, avarice and dread, I promised a great reckoning. I said that the Lord God was with us, that He had asked me to choose a sacrifice because His wrath is powerful and unending. And I made great show, with sly movements of my body and with twists of the arms that I copied from the dancing girls from Cadiz in Cavalcante's castle, and in my hands I held out a narrow bar that to anyone unschooled might seem like a common stone.

And in loud and solemn voice I announced that God would make a sign, that his hand would direct his magical finger towards the chosen sacrifice; and these men were afraid, Brother Andrew was unloosed, I held one arm out wide and the other in front of me, I looked down at the bar in my hand as if I too was afraid of what it might reveal.

I walked forward, into the men. I held my hand flat. And now! I said, the Lord God will point His finger to choose His sacrifice.

The men shrunk away from me, disputing amongst themselves. And the bar twitched and turned and pointed, as I knew it would, to the one who looked as if he had run away from an army because it was the remains of the armour across his shoulder that was attracting the attention of the magnet. His fellows drove him forward.

God has spoken, I said. The axe has been laid to the foot of the tree.

It's a trick! he said. It just points in that direction.

I motioned him to stand on the opposite side, and I held the magnet in my closed hand while he shifted, with the help of his fellows who made a space for him to stand but none for him to flee into. I held the magnet out in my hand again, I relaxed my fingers and let the bar ,turn and again it pointed to the cowardly warrior.

God's finger never lies, I said.

The others gathered around him, ready to seize him, waiting for me to tell them the manner and place of his execution.

And after him, there will be another, I promised.

The designated sacrifice ran out of the door of the hospice, others followed him or threw themselves to the ground, feigned to sleep, or made desperate prayers of obeisance and abasement.

All except for one. The men had been dispatched by my trick, the hospice near empty, some forlorn utensils abandoned in the fright. And there was just one man who was looking at me, from a corner, his eyes wide and shining, a figure so small and quiet that I had taken him for a bundle of rags; he looked like a hunted resolute animal who had found his last corner, which he will fight for.

I asked him in Italian why he did not flee. He answered in English.

Why should I be afraid of a magnet? he said.

We had found the Second Messenger.

His name is Daniel. He holds his left hand closed in a kind of claw, but otherwise he is as we remember him from the friary, a small mouseish boy who had been the uncomplaining mark for Brother Luke's prankish malice and who had lasted longer in the schoolroom than most.

He told us that Master Roger had sent him out a few weeks after our departure.

This is not what I had supposed. I had thought that my Master had grown vexatious after we had gone, and then become inspired, of course, to write more, reconsider some of what he had written, adding further thoughts, withdrawing some previous ones. (And, to my shame, I hoped that he had taken out some words: the writing of Seneca is admirable, but in my Master's humility to the Stoic – and too, in the spirit presumptive he has adopted, of being Alexander's Aristotle, the wise, sometime prolix counsellor – there are passages of the Book that I carry that fall away from perfection.) I had not thought that he had given us so little time to prosper or fall.

The second messenger could not have been constrained as I had been by my companions' penitential conscience. Where we had walked, he must have ridden, or flown. I wondered where it was that he had gone past us.

I would like to see what you are carrying, I said.

It is not for you, he said.

I had supposed that my Master's thoughts had been with me throughout this journey. Lost on the Via Francigena, I had felt the fathering concern of my Master. I realise now that it had been the Book he was concerned for, not its messenger.

You? You are making this journey just on your own?

I had never heard Brother Andrew scoff before.

At the beginning there were two of us. Do you remember Brother Luke?

Brother Daniel was obscure about the loss of Luke. He would not describe how the former tormentor fell by the way.

He fell victim to some disease?

In a way.

We looked at each other, Brother Andrew and I. We were equivalent once more, again depending upon a third to sustain us. What was this mouseish friar capable of? Both of us were questioning this; neither had the answer. Had Brother Luke been abandoned, or rejected? had some heavy ill fortune beset him that his companion had watched, maybe, even, in schoolroom revenge, advanced?

I spoke to him again,

Our Master dispatched you because he was worried that I had failed. I have not failed. We have overcome many obstacles as you must have done. There is no need now for you to proceed. I have found the right road. Viterbo cannot be more than five or six days away. You have done well to get so far, and so quickly. But your mission is over now, you may rest, there are baths in the hillside, which are said to cure all ills, take yourself there, you have deserved it. One day, when my mission is over, when we are all long recovered from our journeys, you can tell me about the end of Brother Luke. The road has marked you as it has us, you can tell me how the road has marked me, or probably there is no need for that, because I will see it in our Master's eyes in the moment of my return.

He watched me talk. I resumed,

You can give me your copy of the Book. I will take that one also, deliver it to its intended recipient. I am sure there are differences between the two versions, my Master's imagination is always restless, but it is not our place to be the judge. We will leave that to the Pope, to whom I will commend your diligence and courage.

The Second Messenger will not be deflected from completing his mission. He will not abandon his journey.

The sun was rising outside. We performed matins together, and then the three of us, ignoring the residents of the hospice, who had great fear of us, went back outside to the day. Brother Andrew retrieved the donkey Bernard from the kind monk. We set off. We walk the same road but not together.

• • •

Saint Ursus's Day

And so we walk, Brother Daniel always ahead. When we rest he rests. When we resume he resumes. If we quicken our pace, he quickens his. He never seems to look behind, but he keeps the same distance between us.

He does not pray with us. He prays on his own. He does not eat with us. Even if he has no food, he will not accept any of ours, our offering dies in the air. When we are having one of our battles with Bernard the donkey, Brother Daniel slows until we have set off again.

He is playing a game with us, Brother Andrew said.

We seem to take it in turns to make remarks that the other fails to show any sign of hearing. We have grown unused to conversation. The donkey Bernard too seems to yearn for a point farther back on the road, like Brother Andrew, who does not answer me as I do not answer him, as Brother Daniel keeps the same distance ahead of us, so that his package is perpetually closer to its recipient than ours.

The way, beaten down to dust by earlier men's feet, winds ahead of us, between tall trees. Beside us, through a knot of branches and thorns, a stream quietly follows the path of our road.

When the road winds away, and Daniel is out of our sight, we no longer quicken our steps, because we know that he will be waiting ahead for us to return into his view.

As we walk on, the stream becomes easier to access. I walk beside Bernard, one hand on his neck, the other on the packages he bears, and Andrew walks beside us, still unglad, but there is a reminder of the joy he has lost in the way he kicks splashing through the water.

And maybe not entirely lost: Brother Andrew smiles at me, and I have not seen his smile since we were enjoying happier days, when his sincere heart was granted its expression. He steps out of the stream, walks swiftly along the bank by the trees, much faster than Bernard and I are travelling, and there is one last sight of him smiling behind the leaves and I can see him no more and I am afraid that he is gone. The road ahead is straight, Brother Daniel walks ahead at his usual distance. He looks behind and around, he is startled, a rustle of leaves, a bird in the trees, a boar or a bear in the woods, and then he resumes his solitary march. I sing. I sing a song my Master and I would sing together.

The road broadens, we are on the approach to a town or a castle. The woods had stretched far, we have seen hardly anyone since day began, a peasant foraging, a messenger on horseback, and in the way ahead, stretching towards a hill, the road is empty apart from Brother Daniel, the familiar brown of his cloak, the tear in it near the shoulders, the bottom part heavy with mud, the package slung over his shoulder; and a figure who is suddenly ahead of him, walking the same distance ahead of Brother Daniel that I am walking behind. In some confusion, Brother Daniel stops. I stop too, with Bernard the donkey. So does Brother Andrew stop up ahead. We stand there, we four figures, pilgrims who have forgotten our destination because we are so fixed on one another. Daniel takes a step forward, as does Andrew in front, as do I behind. Daniel stops, we stop. He walks more quickly to get closer to the one ahead, and I slip away with the donkey from the road into the woods.

I stop my progress to watch him. When he sees that I am no longer on the road, he suffers an agony of choosing. He runs after Brother Andrew and then he stops, looks in every direction, runs back away from him, looking for me, and then towards Andrew again.

When the donkey and I come out of the woods and rejoin Andrew, Daniel is that same distance behind.

He shouts something at us, but the words are lost. I think it is Andrew who sets to running first. We run, even though we first have to pull at Bernard to get him to run along with us, but he takes to it too when he sees there is no danger, that we are not fleeing from enemies – or going to cross water, which he suffers from a dread of doing – but running for the sheer joy of it, his ears rise and fall like wings, and he is faster than we are, which in turn makes us run faster than we thought we knew how. It is not as keen or pure as when I was running down the mountain with Aude my mountain girl, but it is glee all the same, and heart-lifting and joyous, the body sings praise to its Creator when it runs.

We laugh as we run and laugh harder, despite the price as it pulls at our breath choking it in our throats, when we look behind and see Brother Daniel running too, so awkward, like an insect trying to escape a fire. We run until we may no longer run, until our bodies fall laughing and exhausted to the ground. And when Daniel reaches us, he is laughing too, as he falls beside us. And Bernard comes back to rub at Brother Andrew, for whom he has the greater love, and then grazes where we lie.

When we are recovered, after we have drunk in the stream, we share our meal for the day. Brother Daniel brings the food to his mouth with his right hand, because of the perpetually closed claw of his left.

There is brotherhood here, three men and a donkey making the same journey for the same purpose, and it seems foolish to me that we should resist a natural confederacy.

I cannot remember my exact words to him. This is written in a different place, where it is marvellous to be, but I am under an obligation to chronicle how I arrived here. Each minute might seem to be unconnected to every other, but we are all the grateful fulfillers of God's love for us, and everything has been written, everything has been said, if only in a whisper, from the mouth of the Lord.

I said something like,

Come. Let us walk together. Even if we have discord, we are travelling to the same place. Our journey will be a better one if we make it all together.

Brother Daniel has finished eating and he considers what

I have said. He wipes his mouth with the part of his sleeve that is not dusty and torn. He makes no reply, just picks up his package and resumes his walk.

He permits us to catch up with him, and then he stops. We reach him, the donkey Bernard knocks him with his nose as if he too is of our mind and desires unity where previously there has been division. We stop. Brother Daniel takes a step back. He intends us to be walking ahead of him. If we are kept in his sight then he may prevent the guiles that he imagines we desire to play on him.

And so we resume and so we proceed, until night, the company of three followed by the legion of one, whom I have come to hate, his perpetualness, his claw. As we walk I imagine dreadful injuries besetting the body and soul of Brother Daniel.

We made our camp in the woods by the stream. We had drunk from it, Brother Andrew had splashed in it, Bernard the donkey had pissed in it. Despite the heat of the day, the night was cold. Brother Andrew and I curved into each other as we do on the colder nights, and in this silent touch of each other, in sleepy concord, our friendship was closer to what it had been, as if words can separate more strongly than they bind.

My brother Andrew took me by the wrist in the night and woke me. He pressed a finger to my lips and another to my ear. I listened to the sound, which was of feet on the grass, and I thought, as he was thinking, of the Ghibellines, the Blind Monk come to steal the source of greater power than he had wisdom or skill to gather on his own. The night was like a blanket that wrapped around us, befolding our senses, and we shivered, and could hardly move our slothful entwined limbs, and it took longer than it would have at daylight to see and to hear that the sound was not made by the Emperor's wizard or any Ghibelline man, and it was not a beast of the woods, a bear or a wild dog or a snake, or an outlaw or robber approaching with unholy malice. It was Brother Daniel, alone and cold, slipping across the damp earth to join us for our warmth.

And on the following morning, which is the Feast Day of Saint Neot, who was a friend to the poor, and whose relics were stolen from their rightful place, it all resumed as it had the previous day. Bernard the donkey drank from the stream. We gave our separate orisons. When we walked, we walked separately, Brother Daniel following us, determined and alone.

We were a day closer to the Pope. The trees, the stream, the clouds, all seemed brighter, the leaves and water more colourful, their species stronger upon our senses. Every point on the earth is an apex of a pyramid filled with the fires of the heavens. As we drew nearer to the holy father, the heavens burned more brightly.

But we were being followed. This was not the fancy of night, when an insect scratching on a blade of grass becomes a beast in the woods preparing to strike, when lonely Daniel becomes the Emperor's Blind Monk supported by a company of desperate men, when a thought of loneliness, a regret of the passed day, the memory of Aude, becomes a desolating engine powerful enough to dislodge the Almighty One from his throne.

Maybe, I said to Brother Andrew, this is the sickness that ails the lord Cavalcante de Cavalcanti, which I could find no herb to remedy. He is one of the afflicted, who is besieged throughout the day by the thoughts that the Devil whispers to us at night when our defences are so weak.

He did not answer. He is not accustomed to answer me,

and he was listening to the sounds behind us on our path. He stayed the progress of Bernard with a hand to his halter. Brother Daniel saw us stop, so he stopped.

As did our pursuers. We saw their movement more than we saw their shapes, to and fro behind trees by the side of the path behind Brother Daniel.

In our shared peril, we talked again. We discussed our situation without sentiment or pride. There was no discord. If these were pilgrims or merchants whose path happened to coincide with ours, they would not have walked when we walked, stopped when we stopped. We walked on some more until the road had curved, whereupon we drove Bernard complaining into the brambles and hid in the leaves, the stream murmuring beside us, until Daniel had reached the spot on his path which we were hiding beside, and then we gripped him and pulled him towards our hiding place.

He fought against us, he wrapped his arms around his Book, we held on to him. Quickly, because now that we were all out of sight, our pursuers were advancing more swiftly towards us, and they could be seen now, and counted, five of them, in remnants of armour, we strove to reassure him that we were not the ambushers, murder and theft were far from our minds, we were in the same situation as he, the danger was behind us, not before him.

We must leave the road, I said. Cross the stream, find a different path to follow. Whoever these men are, they do not intend us good.

Daniel had always been a quick pupil, and a virtuous one. If he had not, our Master would not have entrusted him with such a precious burden; if he had not, he would not have outlasted, perhaps outlived, Brother Luke. Blessed is the man who resists temptation, for when he has been proved he shall receive the crown of life that God has promised to those that love him. He understood my words and their meaning. He joined us in the thicket as we drove Bernard before us.

Quietly! we exhorted one another, as his hooves dragged in the earth, as he endeavoured to double his weight, to triple it against us, as we heaved him towards the bank of the stream. Our pursuers called out to us, we drove harder at the donkey, who, in his hatred of water, held fast.

His ears were flat back on his head, his eyes wide and long, his hind legs kicking out. I went ahead of him, pulling him by the halter; our pursuers, in confidence, had stopped on the path to watch us.

This is what happened, this is how it happened, we drove harder, Bernard's hooves slid down the leafy slope and Bernard makes a noise I have never heard from him before, that sounds more like a bird's expulsion than a donkey's, and he kicks out with his hind legs and jumps forward with his front legs, and it looks as if he is going to fall, and his eyes open wider, his ears drop back over his skull, but he does not fall over, it is the prelude to running. I try to take hold of his neck but my hands slide back over the coarse hair that cuts into my skin like a thousand needles, so I try to hold him back by gripping on to the packages he bears and I do gain a hold of those, and hug them, but he keeps going, and there is a moment when my feet are off the ground, but I dig in to the ground and hug them even more tightly, and the packages slide away from their straps and drop around me as I fall backwards, and Bernard the donkey, unencumbered, leaps over the stream, bank to bank, without being touched by any of the hateful water, and climbs over the other bank, half-falls, gathers himself, drives through the trees and runs, faster, away.

And we run too, and we lose our pursuers in the woods, but we have lost the donkey, as well as Brother Daniel.

Brother Andrew has gone to look for the donkey Bernard. He has still not returned. I waited for him by the side of the road, the day lingered and fell and he did not return either with Bernard or without him. Neither is Brother Daniel on the same road as me. I proceeded on my journey alone and then I stopped, to wait for my brothers to return, here on the top of a hill where I may see the advance of any other, friend or enemy; but it is all empty, in every direction, and I wonder now if ever Brother Andrew did intend to return, if he would find Bernard, maybe he already has, and the two of them will make their own journey, back to a place of peace and joy.

· · ·

Saint Afra's Day

It is done, I have escaped Brother Daniel, at the cost of losing Brother Andrew; my journey is resumed, its destination not far to reach, and I am alone. Which is a blissful innocent state, that I am taking care not to enjoy too much lest I fall into a kind of voluptuousness.

I set my own pace as I walk, bathe in the stream or not bathe in the stream as I will. My thoughts are my own, taking their time, reaching their end, without deflection or discord. I sing as I walk, my senses expand to fill the air.

Throughout, always, I have been in the company of others, whether it was in the rough hold of my father, or in the company of the villagers without ever feeling that I was truly one of them, and then into the friary, sleeping with the pupils and novices, the days in the schoolroom learning the trivium and quadrivium, the company of my Master and latterly the scribe. And also the company of the other masters, Aristotle foremost among them, and Seneca and Averroes behind, at the head of the supporting teachers of heathen antiquity, with all the saints clamouring for our devotion, and our greatest Master, Jesus Christ, with his blessed disciples, and Francis, the blessed.

Here, the antique voices fade away. I may swing my arms without fearing the injury of another. My thoughts roam where they may.

I remember catching sight of this state when I was a child, away from my father on the hillside, and then in hand-whiles of sloth away from my studies, my Master's thoughts not upon me, when I could wander. In each of these there was an authority near above me, my father's, my Master's, while here I am only beneath God's. Consequently, like the Fathers in the desert, I am closer to Him.

I sing as I walk, and in the sound of my voice in the trees, I hear my lost companions, whom I miss.

The journey I am making now is a mirror of the contemplative journey I took at the friary; and there is another, higher one that mirrors this, from above, and which I was closer to in the schoolroom.

Because, as I approach the end of my journey, it is the journey itself that has become the precious thing, or maybe, merely, just the act of walking. I take a step, and then another, and this could be the eternity that Aristotle teaches, so maybe there is no conflict with scripture, perpetual tread, changing view, in touch with the indwelling divine.

The hills and mountains are behind me. I walked down through the lowlands along a flat way that further descends to a lake. I suppose it is not too late to keep on, walk past

Viterbo, to Rome and on, Jerusalem and beyond, keep walking, one step and then another, until I have found a way to get back home.

• • •

... where I became a pupil, the trivium and quadrivium, which my Master beat into us. As he said, The sword of God's word is forged by grammar and sharpened by logic, but only theology can use it.

These are the elements of the trivium, grammar, rhetoric and dialectic. These are the elements of the quadrivium, arithmetic, geometry, astronomy and music. The walls of my Master's room were dark. Upon them were pages of parchment on which he had inscribed geometrical figures, words from his universal grammar, no devotional pictures. At first there were many of us, sitting in lines, ranked by capacity or, in cases of doubt, age. I began at the end of the last line, but made my promotions swiftly. And as my knowledge increased, as unsatisfactory pupils fell away, I was in the first line, until there was only one line, with Daniel at its head, and me the next beside him; and then Daniel was demoted, after his difficulty with the Hindu numerals passed down by Jordanus de Nemore, and others were gone, and Daniel was gone, and my Master and I were alone with his wisdom, which he poured into me.

My Master was not permitted to travel, but travellers and messengers were permitted to visit him, because he had powerful allies whom the principals of our Order did not dare to oppose. He travelled further in his room than any one could in the world.

There are as many rainbows as men to see them. My Master saw the originals of everything.

We long above all to reach the celestial city. And in the

Spirit he carried me away to a great high mountain, and showed me the holy city Jerusalem coming down out of heaven from God, having the clarity of God, its light like a precious stone, as to a jasper, even as crystal. And it had a wall great and high, with twelve gates, and at the gates twelve angels, and on the gates the names of the twelve tribes of the sons of Israel were inscribed. And the wall was of jasper, but the city itself pure gold like clear glass.

• • •

When I rested for prayer, I made my voice large, to enable God to hear me, who felt so far away.

I called out, out to Him, and to His Son, and to the Virgin, and for the first time in my short, sinful life, I was not sure that They heard me.

But someone had, who was walking along the path that I had taken. He called my name, and it was Brother Daniel, the resolute, the perpetual.

I hated him, and I loved him. I had wished my rival dead, and I held him to my breast like a brother, because it is wrong that we should be so alone.

After prayers, I insisted that we walk together. There had been no need for my attitude of before, we each had a commission to fulfil, that it was the same one should not have wrathed me so, and now it only moved me to regret and shame, that I had been so unchristian and so unbrotherly in my countenance to him.

He suspected me of art, but in his soul I think he was lonely too. So he consented to walk beside me and as we walked we spoke. We shared memories of the schoolroom and sang together songs that our Master had taught us. I told him about Brother Bernard and the changes that he had undergone and the drawings he had made; and in part

I was speaking of this because in the telling my lost brother was brought closer towards me and also because I thought, in the guile that Brother Daniel suspected me of, that if I shared a tale from my road then he would tell me one from his.

But he told me no tales, not about the fate of Brother Luke, nor any other of his adventures, not even the manner of his travels, and nor would he let me see the Book he carried; and at all times he kept his left hand away from me and I suspected that it was not injury that had shaped it into a closed claw but his own will and that there was something that he was keeping hidden in there.

I asked him what he intended after he had delivered his Book. Would he make haste to return to our Master, or had this journey awoken an appetite in him, as I wondered if it had in me, to travel farther? And I started to tell him about the travellers I had met at the castle of Cavalcante de Cavalcanti, but then I fell silent because I was angry with him that all the sharing was being performed on one side only, which was mine; and it was shortly after that we were ambushed.

I do not know how long it was that they had been following us. Perhaps they had been my silent companions for much of the past days, mocking my solitude. But they sprouted up all around us, like baleful shoots of an unholy plant. They were ragged and awful, there was nothing of God inside them, they wore the remnants of battle armour, their modesty was barely concealed, and they carried a Ghibelline flag.

They set upon us, they brought us down, they mocked us, they held the tips of their swords against our skin as they discussed the aptest cruellest ways of slaying us.

They were without compassion or feeling, we were

175

creatures for their sport. They held their blades against our throats so they could see the fear in our eyes. They set us up again, stood in a circle around us, shoved us from one to the other, cutting us, making us fall, until they wearied of this, and some curiosity about us moved them to ask who we were, and whose.

And Daniel, timid Daniel, who hid in the schoolroom, to whom a harsh word would be received as the heaviest blow, called out an imprecation upon them, denied them God's grace, called them tyrants and beasts and monsters, and I wondered if he was doing it to expiate his complicity in however Brother Luke had met his end, and I wondered then as I wonder now if he was doing it to prove himself in my eyes, his new friend, a late becoming.

And at first they laughed at this, as a butcher might laugh at the high spirits of the animal he is herding into the slaughterhouse. They affected respect for him.

But you, my Lord, can grant us mercy and indulgence, said one of them, the leader of this band, whose skin was smeared with dirt and mud, as if he was a creature entirely of earth.

Only if you confess all of your sins, said brave timid Daniel.

And they asked what then, and Daniel said, if they confessed their sins and were truly penitent he had the power to grant an indulgence and a penance and their souls might be spared.

And they acted as if this was a matter of some note for them, and I knew it was only another part of their sport, which they would tire of as they had of the one before, and I looked for escape and found none, and I was wondering if I could break through their ranks and run to safety, and with this I would have the advantage of suddenness at least, and I decided that this was the only way to safety and I would have to try it and I wished for some of Daniel's bravery to wrap itself around me, because I kept forestalling my attempt at escape, telling myself that a better opportunity would arise, while knowing that this was a lie I was guiling myself with. And then I thought about the prophecy that Aude had made, promising my safety, and for the first time I doubted the saint's words.

You are with the Lord? they asked Daniel. You have conversation with him?

I am not worthy, Daniel said.

We will make you worthy, their leader said. We will grant you that blessing.

They mocked poor Daniel, they made as if to pay obeisance to him. They bowed before him, and then they took him to a tree and commanded him to extend his arms out to the side, which he did, and they tied his wrists around the branches of that tree, which were low, but still exerted Daniel to stand on the tips of his toes to avoid his arms being pulled from out of their sockets, and when they had fastened him so, in such a monstrous mirror of Our Lord's own end, they again bowed themselves before him, and asked him, in tones that were high-pitched and girlish, to help lead them out of temptation, into the heavenly paradise that God had promised all faithful men. And this might have been my opportunity for escape but still I did not move, which was not entirely out of cowardice.

And Daniel groaned because of the pain of his enforced position and they affected to believe that he was preaching to them.

What is that, my Lord? Our ears are stopped with sin, we cannot make sense of your words.

And one of them arose, and with his sword, he cut four stripes into the flesh on Daniel's neck and chest, and Daniel shouted out in pain, and his left hand closed more tightly, and the unholy worshippers praised him.

And now I can hear him! one of them said; and the swordsman cut again, and Daniel screamed again, and the unholy band called out in mocking exaltation, *Hallelujah!* and *Amen!*

The sword was thirsty for Daniel's blood. It drank deeply, and Daniel's blood, so red, burst from his skin and dripped down his legs, and made a dark puddle at the foot of the tree, and one of them dipped his fingers into the puddle of blood and made the sign of the cross upon his own forehead, and then the swordsman, as if weary with the sport, swung his arm as if he was about to inflict a blow with all his strength, but then, daintily, pressed the point into the corner of Daniel's right eye, and with a gouge and a turn, he emptied the socket, and Daniel screamed, so loudly that birds flew out of the trees, a wild boar ran from the woods and crossed the path that in our innocence we had been walking a short time before, and the men shouted *Hallelujah!* and *We are surely saved!*

Daniel's empty eye socket dripped blood like martyred tears. The band was losing interest in the spectacle and looking now in the direction that the boar had taken, because they were hungry, as all men are hungry. And the leader said, He is making too much noise now, the sermon is over, and he took out his own sword and drove it into Daniel's chest and dragged it down to his groin, and there was a terrible sound consequent upon it, of a sucking of the flesh that was dying, and Daniel tried to look up to heaven with his remaining eye but he did not have the strength and a terrible sob came from his throat.

He was dying and I had once longed for him dead and I felt shame for this and full pity for him too, who had only

178

found this fate because we share a master who had dispatched us both, and he alone of the two of us had found a strength to confront our persecutors; and I felt envy too, for the agony and passion of his end.

I thought that my own end would be swifter, a colophon, a necessary final office; and I no longer had thoughts of escape, and I cursed them. I promised them all the torments of hell, I told them that the Devil had taken them and he would have his will with them throughout eternity, and maybe because these were to be my last words, or maybe because I was touching some small part of them that was still Christ's, they did not at first interrupt my speech.

But it was interrupted nevertheless, by a call that issued from behind the trees.

Listen, I said, listen to the cries of the damned.

And the sound was a terrible one, that seemed to come from deep in the most awful place, human but not human, full of ugliness and torment.

What is that? one of the men said.

The boar, must be the boar, the leader said. Probably got itself caught.

All the easier to catch then, another said. Our supper is waiting.

I waited for my own end, but the band had gone, I had fallen away from their attention as they went in search of their supper.

The boar must have freed itself, because I did not hear its dying, and nor did I hear the men again.

And although my sorrow for the unjust end of Brother Daniel sustained, my unworthy heart lifted at my own survival, and I gave a prayer of thanks to the angel who protects me.

And then the rain came, to wash poor Daniel clean. I dug a hole in the earth and I laid his body in it, and I pulled apart the fingers of his left hand, and inside it was a rusty nail that he had held, a nail which is the twin of my own one that I carry. I laid it on his heart and covered him with earth. And on his grave I put a cross cut from the tree on which he was martyred.

And I sat there, praying for poor Daniel, and praying for myself, and the rain did not abate, and I did not move from my position even when the rain had soaked my body and my clothes.

And as it is said, King David sat between the two gates; and the watchman that was on top of the gate upon the wall, lifting up his eyes, saw a man running alone. The watchman saw another man running, and crying aloud from above, he said, I see another man running alone. And the king said, He also is a good messenger.

In such a way did come the intercession of the angel who protects me and the martyrdom of poor Daniel.

The Feast Day of the Transfiguration of Our Lord

I am so near my destination and so far away from home, and yet I should not wish for this journey to end. I linger, dally, on this sulphurous hillside. Look away, shut my eyes, and one might think that this will all disappear, and I am sitting at a table, with stern walls around me and the ache of my Master's hand on my head. And yet, the sun on my skin, the rise of my breast with each breath, my eyes closed, and I seem to hear the sounds of my beloved companions restored, which, on occasions, have been so vexing to me, and then I may open my eyes and open my fist and watch a clot of grass and earth fall out of my hand, and I am alone, and the whispering of my companions is only the movement of the wind.

I am accustomed again to carry my own burden. And yet, as I say, I should not wish for this journey to end. Here I lie, with goods scattered across the grass. Above is a village and castle, both named Bullicame. Beneath the castle are sulphur pools where solemn voluptuaries paddle in the mud. Viterbo is not more than five days away.

I have the two books now, and the opportunity to compare them. My Book is fuller, more containing. Daniel's book is hastily done. The sentences are shorter, the book is briefer, it is no advancement upon the Great Work. It is abbreviated, a shadow. Sometime, when I forget myself, I think my master is prolix, saying ten times what he might need only to say once; but a pupil may not judge his master. They are both written by the same scribe and I wonder if even now he is still in my master's room, having given up all thoughts of escape, cutting the words into a third book, a fourth.

The voluptuaries in the sulphur pools are immersed to their broad chests. Their skin is smeared with the mud that is said to have healing powers. Their heads are large and round and correspond to the images my imagination would make of Roman emperors, cruel and orgulous.

It is like the castle of Cavalcante, but it is not like the castle of Cavalcante. There are great men seeking remedy here and lesser men seeking advancement, and weary voluptuaries whose appetites have become diminished through ill use. I was permitted into the library, but the library is neglected. There is a debating room where knowledge, pagan and Christian, is reordered for the sake of disputation and applause. My master charts heaven and climbs closer to God. Here, the primary good is diversion, God is abandoned, His Son bleeds on the Cross and all is subjugated to the tickle of sensation and novelty. Aristotle taught that the quest for knowledge was the highest good. At Bullicame, there is only diversion. Were Bernard here, they would make him lift great weights. Were Andrew beside me they would command him to sing. They find my explanations of things too long and detailed and without the shining novelty that they crave.

The physician here dispenses herbs not for their healing powers but for their abilities to be taken in sweet-tasting wine that transports its drinkers to false perpetual dreams, like the lotus-eaters that Herodotus saw in Libya.

And there are butchers and bakers and common women, who have made another village by the side of the principal one, from which they have diverted the river into a stream to wash their clothes that have been soiled by the tired lusts of the voluptuaries.

· · ·

Saint Laurence's Day

Last night Brother Daniel entered my dreams. I had been delivering justice to my companions of the journey. Brother Andrew was become a ferryman, Brother Bernard appointed to a place of gems and song; the donkey Bernard was given his freedom and released into a field where a female donkey waited to be his dam. Brother Daniel interrupted my tribunal. He was naked and shivering and blood dripped from his wounds. I was angry with him, and I demanded to know what gave him the right to enter my dreams.

My martyrdom gives me the right, he said and instantly I was sorry.

When I awoke, I was shivering, despite the heat of the day. His nail I buried with him. Mine, I pray beside.

The hills and mountains are far behind. I walk down through the lowlands along a path that further descends towards a lake. The sun shines on the water and it is beautiful.

I have learned from Brother Andrew; part of his spirit has entered me, become mine. I hurled myself into the water, longing for immersion. I remained submerged within it until my breath could hold no longer, and I rose, splashing to the surface, breathing great sobs of air, and the water was no longer cold, all was the same, water, and sky and sun, and I felt the lightness of the newly baptised.

I thought I saw someone towards the centre of the lake, yellow hair shining in the sun. I waded further out and submerged myself again; I discovered a small capacity to swim by agitating my arms and legs, but then I could no longer touch the bottom of the lake when I attempted to stand, and this frightened me, so I regained the shallows with much labour and displacement of water, some of which I swallowed.

I looked to where the figure had been but I did not see him; the surface of the water was undisturbed.

Saint Tiburtius's Day

Tiburtius was commanded that he should go barefoot upon burning coals or else do sacrifice to the idols and he made the sign of the cross upon the coals and went on them barefoot, and he said, It seems as if I go upon rose flowers in the name of Our Lord Jesus Christ. And Fabian the provost decried this as sorcery, because, as he said, it was well known that this Jesus Christ was a teacher of sorcery, and Tiburtius was angry at the provost who dared to speak such a holy sweet name, which enraged Fabian the provost, who commanded the head of Tiburtius to be smote off, and in this way was he martyred.

Here in Viterbo, a dreadful melancholy has assaulted me, which I have salved with hellebore diluted with honey, but still I am weary, seem to be on the slope of an abyss.

I found a quiet place on a narrow lane, where I sat and tried to cast my mind back into the friary when I would be contemplating the itinerary map. To imagine myself there imagining this was a greater remedy than the hellebore.

It has been prophesied that this is where I shall meet my death. I may not die. I have my mission to complete. Perhaps this is why I proceed to write, on these last shreds decorated with Bernard's beasts: the tree with the face of the shrew and the tail of a fish, the cloud with the Devil's face, the bush that blossoms wolf-heads for flowers, the dog that walks on its hind legs and has the wings of an angel or an eagle. The author of a chronicle may not die, just so long as he refuses to stop writing.

· · ·

Building works, and men with all kinds of costumes, and crowded lanes, and the companionship of a pale-eyed dog who inexplicably is trying to be my friend, and the street opens into an enormous square like the river finding the sea.

Conscious of my humble state, I waited beneath the steps

along with mendicants and pilgrims and cripples. Some great men walked past us, showed letters of credential to the gatekeeper, were granted admission up to the Loggia, which is a wide stone terrace that looks down over the city walls. We, the humble ones, waited, and some at the head of us were turned away and others joined our numbers, so that by the time the sun had travelled a third of the way across the sky, there were more of us than when I had arrived, and I was further from ascending the stairs.

I do not know if it was a timidity that kept me there so long, or a reluctance to meet the fate consequent upon the ending of my journey, or the knowledge that I would prove to be unworthy of the attentions of the Pope, as well as the trust of my master, but I stood there, with my dog for companionship, pressed by beggars and petitioners and cripples and sleek young men in dark robes who know how to navigate through an ocean of the hopeful towards the touch of the Pope.

A dog may not receive an audience with the Pope. When there was a changing of the guards at the top of the stairs, the ones whose position had been relieved seemed to take delight in driving a rough way through the petitioners, and found sport in hurling kicks and stones at my pale-eyed dog until he fled and another companion had been driven from me. I could see him, crooked and beaten, waiting for me in the centre of the square where the throng was less.

He needed comfort, and his small understanding had settled on me as the one who might provide it. I had even given him a name, Andrew's. But this event, which afforded me the opportunity to delay further the consummation of my mission so that I might provide succour to an innocent, prompted me instead, for reasons I did not understand, to drive on. I took the avenue that the soldiers had opened, and which had not yet been entirely closed. Imprecations attended my progress, which did not abate, rather increased, when I showed my credentials to the guard at the stairs, which granted me access to the Loggia, and then there was a short time watching labourers at work upon the construction of a fountain and the sight through arches of Italy stretching out below, and then a different attendant took me into the Palace, where he instructed me to wait just inside the entrance.

The attendant returned with a Secretary, a narrow man in black Dominican robes who wore no beard but whose face showed the design of it. He studied me without looking directly at me, and hesitated, and read again the Pope's letter to my master with my master's annotations upon it and, finally, seemed to have settled some dispute in my favour, as if his search inside me had been rewarded by the sight of something previously hidden. And I wondered what it was that he had seen, and why he had taken so long to discover it, and which agency had had the power to bury it.

He led me through the Conclave, so much magnificence, where great men sat in the seats carved out beneath wide windows, where craftsmen on ladders painted flowers and lions on the walls, where waiting servants kneeled and great men walked slowly together, circles of power that obeyed their own laws of motion, like the constellations of stars.

At the far end of the Conclave were three stone steps leading up to a wooden door, which the Secretary knocked upon, three quick, almost angry raps that agitated me almost as much as the suddenness of my progress through the Palace.

Wait, he said.

The door opened, and the Secretary went through to the next room, and I waited, tried to form myself in humility and tranquillity as if for a great ordeal. The Pope, more than a king, is greater than a man.

The Secretary returned. He pulled at my sleeve and winced at the touch of it, the lowness of the cloth, its holes and shreds and stains.

His Holiness will see you. Approach his chair with your head bowed. Kneel before him, kiss his foot with due reverence. He will then, if he finds you worthy, command you to stand. Rise to your feet, kiss his ring. Do not initiate any conversation. If he is interested to hear you talk, he will ask you questions.

So much to gaze upon in the next room, a dining table larger even than Cavalcante's in the centre, on which two servants were laying out golden goblets and jewel-handled knives, where the air was scented by glass bowls containing rose petals suspended on water, the colours of all things shifting so I could not tell if the patterns were from the glass or the light shining in shafts through the windows or my own disorder of senses.

We walked through another doorway, into a smaller, square room that I expected to be empty, it should not be so easy to reach the Pope's chamber, it should require more than just the opening of doors. The walls were hung with tapestries red and gold. On one was pictured a Last Supper, Christ flanked by Peter and Paul, trees and vines around them, the celestial city behind them, and, blasphemously, I fancied myself in the picture, with my two companions of blessed memory, resting on our way to the Papal Palace. There was a bed in the middle of the room, covered by a cloth of red brocaded roses, with leaves embroidered in gold and trimmed in green. Red cushions and red carpets, and a servant, whom I at first took for a statue kneeling beside a magnificent wooden throne, the image of a peacock carved on one side, its panels blazing with emeralds and sapphires and pearls.

Approach, the Secretary said.

In all the glory of the furnishings, I had not noticed the man on the throne, who sat there, so slight.

I approached him as I had been instructed to. The ring he offered me was loose and heavy on his finger. Pope Clement, in a larger voice than I would have thought his body could contain, invited me to stand.

I offered him my letter of credential but he did not consent to receive it. The servant rose, poured a glass of wine, which he sipped from, and then wiped the lip of the goblet and bowed, offering it to the Pope, who took one taste from it and placed it with great care and some tremor on the table beside him.

Read it to me, he said.

I did as he instructed and after I had done so, he said,

Your accent is strange. I had expected you to be French. You are not French.

Because this was not a question, I did not say anything in response. The Secretary threw one last suspicious look upon me and left the room, walking backwards. The servant followed him out.

You have come a long way to see me. I hope it is worth it.

I wished to tell him something of my journey. I wished to tell him how changed I have been by it, in ways I still can not understand nor count. I wished to tell him about my brothers, my former companions, the disputes and discords we shared, the love we found. I wished to tell him about

Brother Andrew, his beauty, how all living things love him, and Brother Bernard, who is strong and moody, and yet will weep at the mountains. And I wished for the two of us to make a prayer for poor martyred Brother Daniel, the second messenger. And I wished to take his hand, so pale, so insubstantial, and warm it with mine. Instead, because his remark was not a question, I did not reply to it, following the Secretary's instructions.

You have some things for me, the Pope said.

And I wished to tell him about our adventures as the Pope's Friars, because I hoped they might amuse him.

First take some wine. Then tell me about your master's book, he said.

He shut his eyes when he listened to me talk. I told him about the wisdom of my master, the prodigious discoveries he has made, in so many directions, in the naming and movement of the stars, the reckoning of time, the construction of mirrors and lenses, the secrets of language and life and gold.

All these things are propitious, the Pope said.

And I told him of the falsehoods that have fallen into our translations of the holy books, and about the manufacture of engines of fire.

Your master says you are to perform a demonstration.

I had been carrying an instrument. It, like much else, has not survived our journey.

We will need to be outside, in the sunlight, I told him.

There is a private door in Clement's room, which we had to bow to pass through, the Pope's hand on my arm because he is not strong enough to walk unaided. It took us out on to a terrace, where the Pope, so small, so fragile, seemed to shrink further.

I explained the mechanism, the arm and apparatus that

were missing, I took the lens out from the parchment that I had wrapped it inside for safe-keeping and held it to catch the rays of the sun.

This is a machine for routing our enemies? the Pope said.

A model for a much larger one.

For who has despised the day of small things, the Pope said.

This instrument will harness the sun, I said.

I looked for an object to destroy and chose the shred of parchment. The lens caught the sun and directed it on to the parchment, where the sun's rays gathered on to a small part of the page.

You see how the parchment darkens? This small spot here? It begins to change. Matter will become fire.

The Pope narrowed his eyes, widened them again, and further narrowed them. I hoped this was in response to my demonstration.

All I can see is the outline of some monstrous beast. You saw this on your journey? In a forest maybe?

That is nothing.

Bernard's madness for drawing had polluted many of my pages, including this one.

No, I said. If you look at the beast's paw, there, the page begins to blacken.

Obediently, Pope Clement tried to look past the monstrous drawing on the page. He changed his position. I had to instruct him not to block the passage of the sun's light with his body. He resumed his former position and a cloud passed in front of the sun, and then another.

This is a model only. The final engine will be a hundred times greater.

I am sure it will be glorious, the Pope said to assuage our frustration.

We returned inside. The Pope took his seat again with a heaviness that I did not think he possessed. He rubbed his insufficient eyes.

Here, I will show you, I said.

I held the lens up to him. Look through this, I said.

He looked through the glass. I suggested he move it this way and that to find the best distance of focus and before he was able to see the scorch mark on the beast's paw, his arm lowered: he was not strong enough to hold the glass for long.

I explained how the machine would be erected on a hillside overlooking the armies of the enemy, but I think he was contemplating the ruins of his body rather than the routing of his enemies and my words fell unheeded at his feet.

I held the glass for him and he looked through it once more, this time with his left eye, the other eye shut with one unsteady hand held over it.

I can see you now, he said.

You are very young, he said. Show me your letter again.

I passed him my letter of credential and he read it through the lens that I held for him. He read with delight, not so much as a response to the words on the page but in the joy of a failed capacity renewed.

Your master says you are a virgin, sinless. Is that still the case?

As I tried to compose an answer, the Pope's Secretary came into the room. He knelt before Clement.

We must pursue the work of the day, the Secretary said picking up the first of the letters he had brought in and beginning to read,

Your High Holiness, in sympathy and respect, I offer—

But the Pope interrupted the Secretary.

I shall read them myself, he said.

Clement looked through the glass as before. He had me hold the lens in front of his left eye, and he made some show of finding the best distance from eye to glass to page before reading the letter, saying some of the words out loud in a performance that reminded me of when I was in the schoolroom and we took turns to demonstrate our cleverness.

We will discuss replies later. I still have some matters to transact with this young man.

The Secretary stared at me as he left the Pope's room.

The Pope proceeded to read,

This is the record of the purchase of five parrots from a merchant in Toulouse.

And this is the design for further rooms to be built to the palace.

And these are bills from my physicians.

And this is a pledge of friendship from Charles of Anjou.

And these are complaints about the cruelty and rapacity of Charles of Anjou.

And this is a report of the movements of the renegade Conradin.

This is from an emissary to a Tartar king. We are discussing an alliance against the Saracens.

And this is a statement of accounts of the Papal exchequer.

He looked away from the glass. He dropped the hand that had been covering his closed eye as if he was yielding to a great load.

May I keep the glass?

A sinner may not refuse the Pope. His noble face, like a starving lion's, smiled, and lines opened and stretched on his skin in channels and gullies.

What other miracles do you and your master have for me?

And I told him about some of the engines that my master has written of both in my book and in Daniel's.

I related how my master reveals how to construct an ever-burning lamp, which was the secret lost to the Jews after the destruction of the first temple. And how to make an instrument from a year-old hazel twig that will vibrate to the natural powers of the earth. And how to distil a powder that is antidote to the most deadly snake bite and how to devise weapons of coercion and submission. One, I told him, infuses the air with the heated sap of a plant so your enemies will be stupefied and put to flight. Another is a potion that they may abdicate their will, and desire anything they are directed to. And as well as his burning lens, he has devised other engines of war, flying machines, the consuming fire that no water can extinguish, or the crack louder than thunder that Gideon employed to defeat the Midianites.

These apparatuses are built? or are they children's toys like this other? What is your flying machine?

A mechanical bird, that will enable a Christian to fly over the armies of his enemy.

Is it ready? Has your master constructed it?

Not yet, my Lord. But he will. And he will tell you the recipe for the fire and brimstone of the Lord that rained upon Sodom and Gomorrah.

The attention of the Vicar of Rome, exiled here in Viterbo, falls away. He does not desire possibilities. He is so old, so grey, most of him that is mortal has been purified by illness, the soul preparing itself to quit the body, he is overrun with disease, a besieged citadel stormed by invaders.

And what does he desire, your master? England resists.

Germany will not obey. France sighs and complains. Italy pays nothing, but devours. My treasury is empty.

He only wishes to serve you. He would be Aristotle to your Alexander.

Alexander was young. I do not require a tutor.

He would wish to show you the greatest secrets. He would teach the dignities of Astrology and Alchemy.

Which some call blasphemous novelties.

They are operative and practical; they teach how to make noble metals and many other things better and more abundantly by artifice than they are made by nature. Outside, I saw a colourist painting a vermilion rose. One does not call him a blasphemer for mixing vermilion, which is made from fire and water, sulphur and mercury, which are the components of all metals.

The quickness of my tongue was a marvel to me. I was pleading your case, my master, but there was an ease of companionship between me and this old man, who was the Pope.

Let us eat, said the Pope.

We gave thanks for the food that the servants brought us, which was unbearable, too rich. There were hacks of beef pastured on thyme which clogged my throat with their sinews. Even the white-fleshed bread and the meat of the fish from Lake Bolsena tasted like butter and blood.

Pope Clement hardly ate at all.

And what does your master say about the philosopher's stone? He has discovered this too?

Like the stones that build mountains and palaces, they have contained within themselves all the elements and are called the lesser world. The stone of man, our lesser world, is not a gem or a jewel but blood. This is the secret of the philosopher's stone, as my master will teach you.

And I tried to tell some of what my master has taught about the philosopher's stone, and I included some of his lessons from the book that Daniel was carrying.

Aristotle said to Alexander, I wish to show you the greatest secret, and indeed it is the greatest secret, for not only would it procure the good of the republic and something desired by all by providing enough gold, but what is infinitely greater, it would prolong human life. For that medicine which would take away all dirtiness and corruptions of a base metal, so that it become very pure silver and gold, is considered by the wise to be able to take away the corruptions of the human body to the degree that life would be prolonged through many centuries.

Such a subject has the power to impart its own incorruptibility to other matter – metal or flesh – and to end the incessant warfare among the unequally powerful elemental qualities hitherto resident therein.

As Aristotle has taught us, art can perfect what nature has left incomplete. This is the secret of the philosopher's stone. My master shows how the humours are to be separated. When they have been led back to their pure simplicities by the operations of many difficult works, they are mixed in a recipe that my master has uncovered. He uses quicksilver and calx and blood, incorporated together to make one body.

I had said too many words, I was losing the attention of my listener. He shrank into his throne and closed his eyes. I thought he might be sleeping, but he spoke,

The Psalm tells us, Thy youth shall be renewed like the eagle's... When the eagle grows old, its eyes dim, its wings become too heavy, he seeks out a fountain in which he plunges three times and his wings are light and powerful again, his eyesight restored. He is made new again. Does your master know the whereabouts of this fountain?

As I am still trying to form an answer, he goes on,

Or the bird called the hoopoe. When its father and mother are growing old, it pulls out their feathers, feeds them and warms them under its own wings, until the feathers are grown back, their eyes revived, and they can see and fly as before.

I had not expected a man of such learning as the Pope to believe in this story. It is a fable: Honour your father and your mother. But he is old, and failing, his eyes are dim. Or maybe it is true, it is not a fable, all wonders are true.

My master has enumerated some of the accidents of old age, grey hair and pallor and wrinkled skin and excess mucus and stinking stool, the sickly bleariness of eyes, low blood and low spirits, crabbiness and absent-mindedness, and Pope Clement seems to exhibit them all.

My master, I told him, is hoping to concoct the gloria inestimabilis. Pliny knew of it, as did the saints, prophets and patriarchs. The secret that God told Adam, who lived over nine hundred years. Aristotle tells us that God offers a remedy to temper the humours, conserve health, and defer the sufferings of old age.

You have this? No, you said he was hoping.

It is the medicine of immortality that Homer wrote about. He would concoct it for you and tell you which foods to avoid and which to eat. He would feed you rhubarb and rue, and saffron and gold and coral, and the bone of a stag's heart.

Perfection does not require sustenance, Pope Clement said; and I think he was talking about death.

This holy man, chilled by the accidents of old age and an empty treasury, required consolation, and I had tried to give it to him and we both knew that I had failed.

We had prayed before our meal, thanking God for his foresight, and we prayed again afterwards, Pope Clement's voice profound and wise, stepping out the words like a traveller choosing where to place the stones to make a path over a river. My voice joined with his, softly, without announcement, and it was like being with my master again, the closest I have been with him since I began this journey, music brings us closer than dreams. First he carried my voice along with his, but then I struck out more boldly, found my own path beside his, sometime moving ahead, sometime falling behind, and then hopping forward to join him. I sang without forethought or reason, the habits I formed when I was younger; and his voice moved in response to mine, testing it, finding out how far it could fly ahead or behind, and my voice pulled away ahead of his, because I am young and he is dying, and then I waited for him to catch up with me so we could sing the final verse in step.

Which we did, louder now, obliterating any unhappiness or vexation or sorrow so all that existed was the glory of God, and His creation, manifest.

And then the door was opened and the Pope's Secretary was with us again, and the building of sound that we had built was toppled and Pope Clement was coughing.

The Secretary kneeled before Pope Clement. He held out a goblet of water.

When his coughing was over, Pope Clement pleaded with his Secretary to permit me a little more time with him. He asked me to tell him more about myself and my origins, and I told him about the secrecy of our preparations, the hostage scribe, the suspicion of my master from the other friars, and about my master's goats. And it was only after I had spent some time telling him about the character of each one, and how my master favoured the buck over the wether, and how I had once had to intercede, thrust my body between the she-goat and my master's stick, that I knew I had not been talking about my master at all, that I had never seen my master outside the friary walls, that I had been talking about the man whose face and smell I could no longer remember, who had been my father.

You have warmed me, the Pope said. Where is your book?

In all of this, our fellowship, this brief belonging, I had forgotten the task that had brought me and which had fallen away.

I told him that I had placed it for safe-keeping not far from here. And this was a lie, for I had it in my bag, beside Daniel's. I was crafty in my deceit. I did not reach out a hand towards the bag or even look upon it. I made my great refusal, and my face did not redden.

As it is written, the end of all things will be hastened by the spread of knowledge; and I wished, in my small way, to save my master from his pride that will be the engine of the end times. But he is not my master; I am not his pupil anymore. In this act of treachery I have renounced who I used to be.

You will return tomorrow?

I promised that I would.

And you will give me your master's book. You can remain with us to direct us through the practicalities.

I agreed that I would and my soul was cast into hell with the liars and the perjurers.

I will bring it tomorrow, I said and I knew that I would not. This book is not what the Pope wants or needs. Oh Clement, this book will not save your life, it will not rout your enemies.

In its stead I gave him the strange flower I had found in the mountains that might be moly. I advised him to drink it, the white dried petals, the folded leaves, the black seeds and root, powdered into wine. He took it. I do not think he believed in its efficacy.

Lord, the master of all things, who taught the cock to crow and the cow to milk, listen to my prayer and tell me what I am for.

And I may keep this picture of this beast of yours? And the reading glass?

He picked up the glass again. He held it far away from his face and inspected me.

I bowed my head. I wept.

I do not have to hear your confession. I absolve you, Pope Clement said.

He went out with me, with his arm on my shoulder until the Secretary intervened and performed the office of support to his master. We walked out through the Conclave, and he stood at the doorway as I went out on to the Loggia. He shielded his old eyes against the light.

Forgive me.

• • •

... and in this solitude I have cast off my pupillage and my chronicling, which is, as the saintly girl prophesied, a kind of death. So go, little shreds, and beg your pardon of the Pope, and may you travel safely through Italy and climb mountains and go across the mountains into France, and offer genuflections to the saints, and with safe passage over the water to England, may you make pilgrimage to Oxford and bow your knee and offer greetings from unworthy John, who is no longer a Pupil, and seek the pardon of Master Roger and under his blessed eye there abide.

Afterword

Of the personages within the chronicle:

Brother Bernard's subsequent career is well known and we do not need to rehearse its details here.

Brother Andrew has left behind no mark on the historical record, and, sadly, we suspect his evident frailty did not allow him to live much beyond the time covered by the chronicle.

Of John, we have a little more to go on. He has been identified with the mathematician John of London and the theologian John of Paris. These are plausible but unlikely: John of London was almost certainly born earlier than John the Pupil; and John of Paris was most likely born later, and was a Dominican. It has also been suggested that he might be identified with John of Peckham, later Archbishop of Canterbury, who was definitely a pupil of Roger Bacon's, or have become the explorer to the east known as John Pontecorvo. John of Peckham is much more likely to be the inhospitable former pupil whom our John encountered in Paris. It is possible of course that the truth of Aude's prophecy was actual rather than metaphorical, and that John did meet his end in Viterbo. But, the identification with John

Pontecorvo is the one that we would favour. He might even, after his visit to the Pope, have made his way to Venice to join the expeditioners he had met at Cavalcante's; but that is speculation.

The sickly Clement IV died the following year. His successor was not as indulgent with Friar Bacon or so curious about his researches. In 1272, because of 'suspect novelties', Bacon's teaching was condemned by the Franciscan Order. He was imprisoned. His inventions, discoveries, and rediscoveries – gunpowder, spectacles, the corrected calendar among many others – would have to wait for centuries to be rediscovered. His writings were nailed to the shelves of the friary library: spines turned inwards, they were covered in white cloth and left to rot.

Notes

page xiv
grouped together by ... Yelverton

It is still a mystery through what agency the fragments had found their way into the hands of Yelverton, but he was famous for his avarice for old manuscripts; John the Pupil's chronicle might well have been among the 2,100 codices and codicils collected at the abbey at Bury St Edmunds before being moved by Simon Bozoun in the early 1340s to the (largely uncatalogued) collection at Norwich Cathedral, an unparalleled store of literary treasures, which the rapacious Yelverton was known to plunder. Or, it might have been part of a 'job lot' sold to Yelverton by, probably, a Venetian dealer. This is speculation that offers two contrasting possibilities: in the second, John's chronicle remained in Italy; in the first, the Pupil, or at least his writing, had found a way home.

page 3
... and see your face

This fragment might have strayed from its place in a later passage, the episode of John's lonely reminiscing. However, in the interests of coherence, I have retained its (possibly dubious) place in the narrative.

the friary
The friary here, given its evident rural location, is not the famous Greyfriars at St Ebbe's in Oxford, established in 1224, where Roger Bacon had formerly resided. We do know that four subsequent buildings or tracts of land were given to the Franciscan Order in and around the city. This friary might have been the one for which the Minorites paid an annual rent of one pound of cummin to a certain Walter Goldsmith. Its location and subsequent history are unknown. Contrary to the speculations of most Bacon scholars (see, for example, works by Stuart Easton, 1952, and Amanda Power, 2012), here is proof that Roger Bacon was in England, not France, during this period.

page 5
... Qusta ibn Luqa... Averroes...
These names are significant to an understanding of the transmission of knowledge and philosophy in the medieval period: it was Islamic scholars from the eighth century onwards who had rediscovered Aristotle and the Greeks. The renaissance in learning and investigation in the Christian world of Roger Bacon was reliant on Latin retranslations of Arabic versions of the classical Greeks (and ascribed inventions: the 'pseudo-Aristotle' is one of the most prolific Arabic authors of the period).

page 8
His eyes are the colour of the sea
In the original this is *aqua maris*, that is 'sea water'; but this is problematic, as John surely at this time had never seen the sea. One assumes that he is still following the classical models that had been given him in the schoolroom. One is tempted to write

'blue', but John the Pupil, with his gaze fixed so certainly, behind, on his master, and ahead, on the celestial city, saw the world mostly, I think, in multiple shades of grey.

At the time that John the Pupil was writing, the sky was grey, the sea was green. Blue was just losing its barbarian connotations: Caesar and Tacitus had noted that it was the colour that the Germans and the Celts used for dyeing their bodies to terrify their enemies in battle. And, if Pliny is to be believed, Breton women painted their bodies dark blue in preparation for orgiastic rites. It was the colour the Romans associated with death and the underworld. Blue eyes were a deformity, a mark of bad character.

The three primary Christian colours before the high medieval period were white, which represented purity and innocence; red, the blood spilled by and for Christ, hence martyrdom, sacrifice, and divine love; and black, which signified abstinence, penance, and suffering.

We could go on. We could discuss the Abbot Suger's cathedral of Saint-Denis (completed in 1144), where blue first became the colour of celestial and divine light, and the Virgin Mary's robes, and stained-glass windows and enamelled miniatures, the techniques of woad-dyeing. But if we include these, shouldn't we then mention the trade of the pastel merchants? and the industry of blue in Lincoln and Glastonbury and Picardy and Normandy and Lombardy and Thuringia and Seville? And the madder merchants who tried to besmirch the growing blue industry by employing stained-glass makers to depict blue devils and artists to paint blue hells in their frescoes?

We're not drawing a full-scale map: the notes cannot be as long as the chronicle. (What does it matter that we've done our research?) This is the story of John the Pupil.

And now, he said...

In the original, as we might expect, there is no separation of speech from the main body of the text. Indeed, each chronicle entry is a single undivided paragraph. A more modern usage has been adopted, so as not to deter the contemporary reader.

Ten plus seven.

This refers to the proposed date of John's departure, 17 May.

Saint Brendan

He is the saint later known as 'The Navigator'. One assumes that this first time that John has given us a summary of the acts of the saint whose day it is represents a youthful ambition: he writes of adventures that he hopes will prefigure his own.

The wood of the cross...

The opening of this passage has undeniable echoes of Jacobus de Voragine's *The Golden Legend*, the early-thirteenth-century compendium of lives of the saints, as do some subsequent passages in the Chronicle. This should not surprise us: in the scholastic era, as the historian Jacques Le Goff reminds us (see, for example, *Les Intellectuels au Moyen Âge*, 1957), the idea of authorship was very different to ours; God was the only true author; texts, *pace* Barthes *avant la lettre*, were tissues of quotations from Scripture, from the commentators, from oral and written fables, from the classics of the ancient world (see the *Papers from the Annual Proceedings* of the 10th Intertextuality Conference, Canterbury, 2011, particularly those contributions from Miller Bovey, Thomas Sackville, Amanda Novillo-Corvalán, et al.). As for lawyers at the very highest court, all was precedent, in the wait for Judgement at the end of time.

It is unclear whether this passage was written as a response to the early rigours of the journey, as notes for a sermon, or just as meditation: the medieval clerical mind apprehended at least four simultaneous planes of meaning: the literal, the allegorical, the moral, and the eschatological. So, for example, John's journey was an actual one; it was also a walk in Christ's footsteps, towards the celestial city; as his soul moved closer to God, away from sin; and it was conducted in the light and darkness of the Final Judgement and impending End of All Things.

page 25
Towards the end of the day
When trying to calculate the distances the companions travelled, and their likely or possible stopping points, we must remember that among the many differences between them and us was their greater hardiness and stamina. On sometimes difficult terrain, in unforgiving footwear, they would have travelled an average of over thirty miles a day. Their first day of walking would have taken them deep into Berkshire.

page 30
the trouble in Rochester
What the 'trouble' might have been is unknown. Most of the journey from the Franciscan house just outside Oxford to Canterbury is missing in the manuscript. And this 'trouble' is hardly alluded to later on.

page 48
I did not explain... there are novelties...
This change of tense is typical of John's prose. Maybe these descriptions were written quickly, maybe he is not as commanding of

language as he would claim to be – because, in these early passages at least, sometimes breaking through his preferred tone of modesty and humility, there is a sort of quiet boastfulness, pardonable of course in one so cloistered and young, whose aptitude for the reception of his Master's learning was not just a cause of intimacy between teacher and pupil but a matter for performance, to demonstrate both his master's pedagogy and his own capacity to receive it.

page 52
In such a way did we effect our first escape
Glossing over some uncertainty over this episode – and were not John exercised upon a sacred trust, we would speculate as to whether he is embroidering or partly inventing a story that demonstrates his capacity on the road – we need to draw attention to this final sentence of the day's entry.

The impression given, sometimes overtly, is that John is writing his account of the day shortly after the events he describes – sometimes indeed he seems to be writing his Chronicle *during* the events: the companions break from their walk and John takes out his scribe's paraphernalia and cuts his words into the page (see, for example, p. 55: 'I write this through the dirt of the road'; p. 101: 'cutting these marks'). Sometimes his discourse takes the form of an imaginary letter to his master, the friar Roger Bacon, sometimes a sermon, sometimes a rudimentary kind of history, but always the same impression is given: John is making his account shortly after the events he is describing.

Here, however, we have a troubling anomaly: how can he know that this is the companions' *first* escape from Simeon the Palmer? There are two alternatives: did he add this last line sometime afterwards? which would indicate a greater artifice to the composition than its naive tone would indicate; or is much of the

Chronicle or even its entirety written at a greater remove than it would seem from the events it describes? (John's frequent, maybe over-frequent, use of the historical present tense is not unknown to his times, but is not found anywhere in the chronicles of his countrymen Jocelin of Brakelond and Matthew Paris.)

Similarly, in his later account of his visit to the village of the saint, the time that elapses (three days at most: 21 to 23 July) doesn't seem sufficient to allow for the days and nights that John describes.

I have only once seen, and all too briefly, the original manuscript. Without being able to examine it further, these questions remain unanswered, and unanswerable. There is of course a third alternative, which is even more troubling.

page 56
engendered a race...
The reference is to Genesis 6:4.

page 60
and the people feast and dance
This suspicion of dancing was often recorded. Contemporary to John the Pupil, the Dominican preacher Thomas Cantimpratanus wrote: 'If it be better to plough on a Sunday or holy day than to dance; and if servile works, such as ploughing, are a mortal sin upon holy days, therefore it is far more sinful to dance than to plough. Yet those dances which are held at the weddings of the faithful may be partly, though not wholly, excused; since it is right for those folk thus to have the consolation of a moderate joy, who have joined together in the laborious life of matrimony.'

page 61
this walled town
This is perhaps Beauvais, whose walls date from Roman times,

and whose cathedral was, until its collapse in 1284, the tallest in Europe.

page 63
At the suburbs of Paris...
The manuscript is particularly fragmented in the Paris sections (and there is a possibility that they are an amalgam of *two separate* episodes – perhaps the companions returned briefly to the city in their period of being lost – which would explain some of the apparent inconsistencies in the translation). I have taken the liberty of removing an extended discussion of the science of optics, which makes little sense in its present state. There is a possibility that portions of the Paris section (or sections) have been deliberately suppressed by followers of John's predecessor, the Master's earlier pupil, whom we might identify tentatively as John of Peckham, the future Archbishop of Canterbury, to protect the reputation of his later years.

page 73
Thrust, tongue...
A gross parody of the first verse of Thomas Aquinas's poem/hymn *Pange Lingua Gloriosi Corporis Mysterium*:

> *Pange, lingua, gloriosi*
> *Corporis mysterium,*
> *Sanguinisque pretiosi,*
> *quem in mundi pretium*
> *fructus ventris generosi*
> *Rex effudit Gentium.*

more usually translated along the lines of:

> *Acclaim, my tongue, this mystery*
> *Of glorious Body and precious Blood*

Which the King of nations shed for us
A noble womb's sole fruitful bud.

page 73
the Pope's Friars
The legend of the Pope's Friars, or Magicians, is a verified one:
two of the poems collected in Helen Waddell's *Medieval Latin
Lyrics* (1929) refer directly to it.

page 75
The woods are thick
They are, presumably, lost in the Clairvaux Forest.

page 76
the twentieth book
In fact, Augustine relates this story in the twenty-second book of
De Civitate Dei. John's normally reliable scholarship, or memory,
fails him here.

?
This modest but opportune punctuation mark is John's own
invention (although it might have been the result of a smudge
from a fire or a careless slip of Gerald Lovelace's knife or, conceiv-
ably, an erratum introduced in the transcription stage by the
modern scribe who, like Roger Bacon's own, will have to remain
perpetually unknown), the use of which the editor has gratefully
adopted.

page 77
Abelard's great enemy
A reference to the proselytiser, and mystic, Bernard of Clairvaux.
Abelard is of course Peter Abelard, the great twelfth-century
logician.

page 78

Via Francigena

The road they are following is the traditional pilgrim and merchant route from Canterbury to Rome. Notable points along the way would be: Dover, Calais, Arras, Laon, Reims, Châlons-sur-Marne, Bar-sur-Aube, Clairvaux, Langres, Beaune, Besançon, Pontarlier, Chambéry, Mon Cenis, and then into Italy: Moncenisio, Aosta, Pavia, Piacenza, Berceto, Certaldo, Pontremoli, Lucca, Siena, San Quirico, Bolsena, Viterbo.

We should note that this was not a single road. For example, the companions crossed the Alps at Mon Cenis; other travellers on, nominally, the same route, went into Italy by way of Switzerland at the Great San Bernard pass.

page 83

Brother Bernard is suffering... demons...

It seems obvious to us that Bernard's sickness is due to an infection contracted from the filthy rag he had been gagged with: but their times are not ours, and they are not us; the companions had a different notion of cause and effect, despite Roger Bacon's efforts to unite them: in the gaps between events were angels and demons.

This raises a historiographical point, which belongs somewhere, so I shall place it here. There are some who still believe in an unaltering substance called 'the human condition', as if we can know Bernard, or John, as if we could think like them, might even somehow become them. But the past is eternally different from us. That is why all historical novels are failures or, at best, metaphors, dressing up the present day in anachronistic disguise. To think we can gain a better understanding of ourselves by studying our precursors with curiosity and sympathy is tempting, but you are not I, and I am not John the Pupil, no matter how much I yearn to be; all metaphors are suspect. This is above all why we are so grateful to the collector for allowing us access to an actual past.

It was like the window we saw
Presumably a reference to the 'Rose Window' of the cathedral at Reims.

page 89
Bernard's designs
Bernard's doodles might have been lost in a library fire or had their lines scratched away and washed clean so the parchment could be reused. They might have been consumed by mould or chewed away by silverfish and cockroaches and lice; they might just have been discarded, tossed aside by a careless owner who had no thought for what he had. It is possible that they were torn up and used in the binding of a book, as pastedowns or backing in the spine or cover, to be disinterred by a lucky reader inside an antique breviary or bible.

page 90
with whom Brother Andrew...
It is unclear whether the omitted words here are due to a break in the manuscript or to the modesty of John the Pupil.

We have lost our way
By now the companions are somewhere in the Burgundy region, perhaps in the vicinity of Beaune or Chalon-sur-Saône.

what happened to Brother Andrew
Again, we can only speculate what happened to Andrew, who seems particularly prey to injury and assault.

page 93
The gardener is Father Gabriel
The medieval clerical mind appreciated gardens, and not just for the principles of divine harmony and proportion they could exemplify – Jesus spent the night before his arrest in the garden

at Gethsemane; Augustine experienced his conversion in a garden at Milan. Frustratingly though, much of this episode is lost, as is the garden itself. It grew somewhere in the foothills of the French Alps, but there is no record of it, and no vestige, as its gardener so evidently feared.

A further question arises: we remember that John the Pupil's chronicle is a record of temptations and trials. What then is undergone here? It is hardly a trial for him to be in a garden, lovingly and wisely tended. Is it the test of loyalty to Master Roger? of whose knowledge and wisdom John is at last beginning, if not to doubt, at least to sense the limits; is it the temptation to remain in this place, to abandon his mission for a man who, no matter how kind and wise he is, may only prove to be another false father? Is it the sin of pride that John is committing by presuming to be the future gardener of a new Eden? The collector has a different theory, but I have no interest in his somewhat prurient speculations.

page 96
You are the seal of the image of God...
An odd quotation for John to make in this context; and he has made it earlier in his Chronicle (p. 38): it comes from the book of Ezekiel (28:12–13), describing Satan before his fall that prefigured mankind's own.

page 106
her native language
Which is presumably Occitan, the old language spoken either side of the Alps and Pyrenees.

page 112
There is a monastery on the very top
This is probably the Sacra di San Michele, which, despite Brother Bernard's silent scorn, was Benedictine.

I am no better than the men of Sodom

The reference is to Genesis (19:1–10), in which the lascivious men of Sodom betrayed all traditions of hospitality to the visiting angels, by demanding that they be expelled from Lot's house, 'so that they may know them'.

These will be my final references to the collector, other than to praise him for enabling this document to be, but it is quite wrong, of course, to look at the 'relationship' between John and the mountain girl from the perspective of twenty-first-century manners. Unlike our benefactor, I am sure that there was no sexual relationship between the two, which might account for her rather snappish remark that he 'would prefer her sister'. One of John's qualifications for delivery of the book was that he was a virgin. Without doubt, something occurred between John and his mountain girl, an accord, a sympathy, an affinity; this does not mean that they made love.

Similarly, the modern reader may be unnecessarily tempted, as the collector has been, to draw anachronistic conclusions about the nature of the 'warming' that John performed on Andrew's body (p. 109).

The battlements of their cities are carved like swallows' tails

The Ghibellines were the party of the Holy Roman Emperor. Their emblem was, as John writes, a red cross on a white background. The Guelphs, the party of the Pope, had a white cross on a red background. Ghibelline cities and castles were distinguished by the shape of the merlons at the top of their battlement walls, which were cut into two triangles that indeed are reminiscent of a swallow's tail. Guelph merlons were rectangular.

By 1267, the Ghibellines were in retreat. Frederick II was dead, his successor Conrad was dead; the emperor was now the sixteen-year-old Conradin, Frederick's grandson. In little more than a year, Conradin would be captured and executed, Rome would be restored to the Pope, and subsequent internecine squabbling would be between the so-called 'White' and 'Black' Guelphs. But in 1267, Italy was still in a state of civil war.

page 117
It is a hillside village like any other
This is another fragmented episode. The reason for this could easily be ascribed to the depredations of time and ill-use; but there are other possible causes. John might not have had the time or attention or placidity of mind to compose an entry as assiduously as we have become used to expect. It is also possible that John might have removed passages from this episode himself, to spare a judgement upon the 'saintly girl', or maybe even upon himself. This would be untypical though: up till now, John has been seldom if ever sparing of anyone's blushes, especially his own. His halting candour makes us admire him more.

As to where and who, this is problematic: the shape of John's journey – he would be at this point between Lucca and Florence – puts the 'hillside village' somewhere around Pistoia, in Tuscany. Aude is clearly one of the so-called 'Tuscan lay saints' who were active during this period. One might make a tentative identification with Margherita of Cortona, whose first hagiographer, the Franciscan friar Giunta Bevegnati, wrote, 'No one was ever so greedy for gold as Margherita was to annihilate her body.'

page 130
The boy knight ... named Prince Guido
Of all the characters whom the companions encounter, their impetuous rescuer, Guido Cavalcanti (*c.*1253–1300), is the one who has been most remarked by posterity. This is partly because of his own poetic genius (with notable translations by Rossetti

and Pound among many others), but largely because of his luck or otherwise in his 'first friend', Durante degli Alighieri, more commonly known as Dante.

Guido's father, the kindly freethinker Cavalcante de Cavalcanti, was placed by the poet in his *Inferno*, in the sixth circle of hell, reserved for heretics; he is perpetually anxious for his son, who, Dante implies (Canto X), will soon be there to join him – a malicious sly prophecy which came true: Guido died of malaria shortly after Dante wrote these words; the disease was contracted in the swamplands of Sarzana, an exile that his former 'first friend' had condemned him to.

It may be coincidental to this falling-out of friends that Guido's wife was named Beatrice.

page 153
Chi è questa che vèn ...
This early poetic triumph by Guido Cavalcanti, and one that previous commentators have failed to register as displaying a direct Baconian influence, has as its first two lines:

> *Who is she that comes, that everyone looks at her,*
> *Who makes the air tremble with clarity?*

page 172
the eternity that Aristotle teaches
Aristotle's theory of the eternity of the universe, with no beginning or end, in contradiction to Christian doctrine, was answered by the Condemnation of 1210, which banned his books from the University of Paris. When the philosopher was reinstated a generation later, and there were no Frenchmen schooled to teach him, lecturers, including Roger Bacon, were brought in from Oxford, in the early 1240s.

where I became a pupil

This passage might well be part of the same as the opening
section – only a melancholy in its tone suggests that it belongs
here, after the loss of Brother Andrew. Conversely, the opening
section might be part of this one.

And in the Spirit ...

John is quoting here, in abridged form, from The Apocalypse of
Saint John (Revelation) 21:10–18.

page 181

I have the two books now

John's book is Roger Bacon's great (and sometimes rambling) work,
the *Opus Majus*. Immediately after John's departure, or perhaps even
before it, his master set to work on another, the abbreviated version
that Daniel had been carrying, which he called the *Opus Minus*. As
John surmises, there is also a third version, a kind of introduction
to the first two, called the *Opus Tertium*. It is as if, restricted to his
tower, unable to hasten or influence the path of his book to its
intended reader, all Bacon could do was to keep composing, and
dispatching, increasingly miniature versions of his great work.

page 182

They find my explanations of things too long

There seems to be something John is not saying here, or many
things (and it makes us reconsider what we noted earlier about
his candour): what is his business in Bullicame? He implies that
he is a guest here, and appears to have the run of the place to
wander through; but along with his disapproval there seems to be
a resentment. He notes that if Bernard were there with him, he
would perform feats of strengths. If Andrew were there he would
be singing. John himself implies that he bores his audience with

his speeches, so it is not too big a jump to assume that John was there only as a kind of performer, and not a popular one at that. He also seems to have a knowledge of the 'common women' (i.e., prostitutes), so it is possible that it is with them he had been billeted. His scornful remarks about the disputes run for entertainment at Bullicame might suggest his failure at competing in them.

John was longer at Bullicame than this fragment would indicate: in 1267, the Feast Day of the Transfiguration of Our Lord fell on 6 of August; his next entry, Saint Laurence's Day, would have been written for the 10th; but Bullicame is only a day's walk from his next stop, Lake Bolsena.

At the beginning of his chronicle, John had seemed to be aiming at an inclusivity of consideration. His perceptions were constrained by his inexperience and piety, so, in the early sections for example, he hardly bothers with physical description (which would be in keeping with the typical clerical attitude of *contemptus mundi*, that is, a contempt for the base fallen matter of physical reality) but he doesn't seem to be holding anything back. By now though, he has matured as a writer, even if his artifice, or self-editing, can be guilelessly clumsy.

page 184
Building works ...
From my one encounter with the original manuscript (and, in our gratitude to the benefactor, we must pardon his jealous ownership), I have seen that the visit to the Pope is on one unfragmented quire of parchment, which suggests that it was written later.

We can easily imagine that, after the events, John might have been looking through his rough chronicle and making changes, keeping to the manner of an account by a witness when, in fact, he was recollecting the entire expedition from a farther vantage point. I have to confess now that I have wondered if the first-person narrator is a kind of fiction, that the whole thing was composed by the lonely magus Roger Bacon in his prison seclude, deprived of his books and his instruments but driven, as ever, to lecture and elucidate, but this time casting his theories in a more immediate mode than his customary discourses of philosophy and theology could afford; and, further, if this theory is allowed any credence, that it was also a kind of ruthless *mea culpa*, an accusation to the self that he had cast his cherished pupil on to turbulent tides for, really, the purpose of his own fame and preferment. In all Bacon's recovered writings, it is only in reference to John – 'a virgin, not knowing mortal sin ... full of sweetness, goodness and discretion ... and an excellent keeper of secrets' – that he allows himself to express, or maybe even to feel, any fondness or tenderness for another human being.

ABOUT THE AUTHOR

DAVID FLUSFEDER was born in New Jersey, but has lived most of his life in London. He has published six novels, including *The Gift*, and is currently finishing an opera. He has been a television critic for the *Times* and a poker correspondent for the *Sunday Telegraph*. He teaches at the University of Kent, where he is the director of creative writing.